BERNIE & MAGRUDER
& THE DISAPPEARING BODIES

BERNIE MAGRUDER & THE DISAPPEARING BODIES

Phyllis Reynolds Naylor

ALADDIN PAPERBACKS

New York   London   Toronto   Sydney   Singapore

First Aladdin Paperbacks edition April 2001

Copyright © 1986 by Phyllis Reynolds Naylor

Aladdin Paperbacks
An imprint of Simon & Schuster Children's Publishing Division
1230 Avenue of the Americas
New York, NY 10020

Originally published as *The Bodies in the Bessledorf Hotel*
The text for this book was set in Adobe Garamond.
Printed and bound in the United States of America
10 9 8 7 6 5 4 3

The Library of Congress has cataloged the hardcover edition as follows:
Naylor, Phyllis Reynolds. The bodies in the Bessledorf Hotel.
(Bernie Magruder mysteries)
Summary: Dead bodies which appear and disappear mysteriously are threatening to lose Bernie's father his job as manager of the Bessledorf Hotel. What can be done? How do you find a ghost?
[1. Mystery and detective stories]
I. Title. II. Series: Naylor, Phyllis Reynolds.
Bernie Magruder mysteries. PZ7.N24Bn 1986 [Fic] 86-3602
ISBN: 0-689-31304-7 (hc.)
ISBN: 0-689-84127-2 (Aladdin pbk.)

For my special friends,
Eric and Jeremy Bono

Cigars and Citronella

The Bessledorf Hotel was at 600 Bessledorf Street between the bus depot and the funeral parlor. Officer Feeney said that some folks came into town on one side of the hotel and exited on the other. The Bessledorf had thirty rooms, not counting the apartment where Bernie Magruder's family lived, and Feeney said that there could be a body in any one of them.

"You know where most folks die, Bernie?" Officer Feeney said one morning as Bernie walked to the park beside him.

"On the highway?" asked Bernie.

"Nope."

"Airplanes?" Bernie guessed.

The policeman shook his head. "Most people," he said, swinging his nightstick, "die in bed, which goes to show that bed is about the most dangerous place you can be."

Bernie had never thought of that before.

When they stopped at the light on the corner, Feeney glanced back over his shoulder toward the hotel.

"Thirty rooms, times 365 days, makes about . . . oh, ten thousand folks coming and going in a year," he said. "And out of ten thousand folks, chances are that at least one of 'em's going to die at the Bessledorf."

Bernie had never thought of that either. Officer Feeney was always digging up things for Bernie to worry about in the middle of the night.

Of course, there weren't ten thousand people staying at the Bessledorf in a year. For one thing, not all the rooms were filled unless there was a convention in town. And second, some people actually lived at the Bessledorf, so there wasn't as much coming and going as Feeney imagined.

Old Mr. Lamkin, for instance, had lived at the Bessledorf since the day his Dodge gave out. Folks said the old car broke down in the middle of Main Street and wouldn't go backward or forward. Lamkin got out, walked around it as though it were a wounded elephant or something, poked around under the hood, and then just walked off and left it, got a cab to take his belongings to the Bessledorf Hotel, right on a bus line, and hadn't set foot in a car since.

Mrs. Buzzwell was another regular. Mrs. Buzzwell had a voice like gravel going down a tin chute and a mouth that was always busy. She had moved to the hotel the day after her husband died, and everyone said if she'd moved the day *before,* he might not have kicked off at all.

As for Felicity Jones, she stayed at the Bessledorf, she told them, because she had such a marvelous view of the moon rising over Bessledorf Hill that it inspired her to poetry. She could not, she insisted, ever bear to leave.

The Magruders lived at the Bessledorf because

Theodore, Bernie's father, was manager. Before that, Mr. Magruder had been a house painter, an auctioneer, and a vacuum cleaner salesman; and the four Magruder children had been drifting around the country like dry leaves on a windy day, as Mother always said. Now that they were here in Middleburg, Bernie hoped they would stay.

It was a cozy sort of town, just the right size, Bernie thought. When he stood at the front door of the hotel and looked straight ahead, he could see City Hall. If he looked to the left, he saw the newspaper office at the end of the street. If he looked to the right, he could see the parachute factory at the top of Bessledorf Hill. And if he walked around the block with Officer Feeney, as he often did on Saturdays, they ended up in Middleburg Park, where there was a creek. The creek became a stream, the stream became a river, and Bernie thought that Middleburg was the best place to live in the entire state of Indiana. Until Feeney started talking bodies, anyway.

"How many dead people have *you* seen?" Bernie

asked Officer Feeney as they walked around the fountain in Middleburg Park.

"Half dozen, I suppose," said Feeney.

Bernie had only seen one, and that was through the window of the funeral parlor next door. "What do they look like, really?" he asked.

"Same as when they were alive, but a bit more relaxed," Feeney told him.

Bernie was still thinking about bodies when he got back to the hotel. He stepped over Mixed Blessing, the Great Dane who was asleep on the mat, picked up his two cats, Lewis and Clark, said hello to Salt Water, the parrot, and went back to the apartment behind the lobby. Joseph, Bernie's older brother, often brought home animals that had been left on the steps of the veterinary college where he went to school. If the lobby of the Bessledorf Hotel sometimes resembled a zoo, it was because the Magruders, having been drifters themselves, could not bear to turn the animals out.

Mr. and Mrs. Magruder were having a conversation in the kitchen when Bernie entered. It may have been a conversation to them, but it was an argument to Bernie.

"Heliotrope," said Bernie's mother.

"Cigars," said his father.

"Wisteria and citronella," said Mrs. Magruder.

"Old T-shirts," said Mr. Magruder.

Bernie wondered if he should get involved or eat a bag of pretzels. He reached for the pretzels.

"But who . . . ?" Mother continued.

"Someone who upsets my digestion, that's all I know," said Father.

"What are you talking about?" Bernie asked finally.

"A man who checked in yesterday," said Mrs. Magruder. "I don't know what it is about him, but he reminds me of citronella and porch swings."

"He reminds me of stale beer," said Bernie's father.

Mother wrote romance novels in her spare time, and it wasn't at all unusual to hear her talk about porch swings and citronella. But there was something here more unsettling than a romance novel, and Bernie knew better than to get mixed up in a crazy argument like this. It was only nine-thirty on a beautiful Saturday morning, and he had been thinking of calling up his friend Weasel, or maybe Georgene Riley, to go skateboarding on Bessledorf Hill. He'd been thinking, actually, of starting at the top to see just how far he could go. If he could pass the bus station and the funeral parlor and roll all the way down to the newspaper office without falling off, he just might possibly get his name in *The Guinness Book of World Records.*

At that moment, however, there was the sound of hurried footsteps outside in the lobby, a knock on the apartment door, and Hildegarde, the cleaning woman, burst into the kitchen, her eyes as large as pancakes and her face the color of library paste. Her red hair seemed to rise right off the top of her head as she tottered across the floor, bumped into the refrigerator, and went reeling back in the other direction.

"Hildegarde!" cried Mr. Magruder. "What is the matter?"

But Hildegarde couldn't speak. One hand rose to her throat and she ran to the door once more and pointed to the lobby, her mouth opening and closing without a sound.

Mrs. Magruder took her arm and helped Hildegarde to a chair. "You have had a terrible fright, my dear," she said, her own voice rising. "Try to calm yourself and tell me what on earth in heaven's name has happened?"

Hildegarde's eyes seemed to roll around in her head.

"A body," she gasped finally. "Died right there in the bathtub, he did, with all his clothes on."

2

The Body Snatchers

"Hildegarde, what are you talking about?" asked Father. "Sit down and tell me exactly what happened."

The cleaning woman hunkered down into a chair and hugged herself with hands that were shaking.

"I makes the bed in 107," she told him. "I dusts the dresser, vacuums the rug, then picks up my bucket and goes into the bathroom and there . . . sticking over the edge of the tub, was this foot . . . in this shoe. . . . And when I peeks in the tub, here was this face. . . ." Hildegarde rolled back her eyes and let her tongue hang out as a demonstration.

"We have got to stay calm," said Mrs. Magruder,

as she paced the floor. "We absolutely must keep our wits about us," she added, biting her nails. She grabbed Hildegarde by the shoulders and shook her back and forth. "We cannot afford to be hysterical!"

Awakened by all the commotion, the three other Magruder children came wandering into the kitchen: Delores, the oldest, who was twenty; Joseph, who was nineteen; and Lester, nine—just two years younger than Bernie. They stood sleepily there in the doorway, rubbing their eyes.

"What's going on?" asked Delores, yawning. "There's enough noise out here to wake the dead."

"Don't *say* that!" shrieked Mrs. Magruder.

"Has something happened we should know about?" Joseph asked.

"There is absolutely nothing to get excited over," Mrs. Magruder told them. "Nothing at all. Hildegarde has found a body in the bathtub, that's all."

"In *our* bathtub?" asked Lester, looking around to see if any of the family was missing.

"Listen," said Mr. Magruder. "Somehow we have to get the body out of there without alarming the other guests. Bernie and I will stroll leisurely down to room 107 and wait until the police arrive. Alma, my dear, call Officer Feeney and ask him to come in the back door. When he has written up his report, I will see if we can't wrap our departed guest in a bedsheet and wheel him out in a laundry cart. The worst thing that can happen to a hotel is to have someone die in one of the rooms."

Mrs. Magruder went to the phone and dialed headquarters, and Bernie went out into the lobby with his father. Following at a distance was Delores with her hair in curlers, Joseph in his plaid robe and fuzzy slippers, Lester eating Rice Chex from a box, and Hildegarde sniffling and snuffling into her handkerchief.

As the procession crossed the lobby, the Great Dane, Mixed Blessing, tagged along and the cats joined in. When Bernie turned the corner and started down the hall, however, he saw a small crowd standing outside the door of 107.

There was old Mr. Lamkin, wearing his raincoat over his pajamas; Mrs. Buzzwell in her green flannel gown; and Felicity Jones, who leaned weakly against the wall, looking pale and frightened.

"Good morning!" said Mr. Magruder brightly. "Isn't it a fine morning? A beautiful morning, in fact!"

"What is it, Magruder? Murder or suicide?" asked Mr. Lamkin. "Has anyone found the weapon?"

"What are you talking about?" asked Bernie's father.

Mrs. Buzzwell folded her arms across her chest. "The minute I heard Hildegarde go running down the hall, I knew that something was wrong. First thing I did was wake up Miss Jones and Mr. Lamkin, because whatever happened to that poor soul in room 107 could happen to us all."

"My dear Mrs. Buzzwell, you are truly a model of alacrity and vigilance," said Mr. Magruder. "What has happened in room 107 is just one of life's little misfortunes, but I assure you that we shall dispatch the occupant with as much dignity as we would afford a member of our own family."

"Who did it?" asked Mr. Lamkin. "The handy-man? The cook? Anybody check for fingerprints?"

"I've already composed a poem to be read at the funeral," said Felicity Jones:

"What beastly deed has robbed us thus
Of neighbor 107?
Weep, O angels, fold thy wings
And welcome him to heaven."

Hildegarde, at the end of the procession, began to sob.

"Bernie and Joseph," said Mr. Magruder. "Come in here. The rest of you please wait out in the hall."

Bernie and his older brother followed their father through the doorway. Bernie swallowed. He had never been this close to a corpse. He was afraid he might see a bullet hole in the head or a wound in the chest. Blood all over the floor.

"I need you both as witnesses," Mr. Magruder told them. "Don't touch a thing, but take a good look around. Then, if there are any questions later, perhaps we'll know the answers."

While Mr. Magruder and Joseph scanned the room, Bernie got down on his hands and knees and looked under the bed. Nothing there but a few dust balls, a pair of brown slippers, and a gum wrapper.

They prepared to enter the bathroom. Mr. Magruder stepped across the threshold, Bernie beside him, Joseph peering over his left shoulder.

Bernie gasped. There was no shoe, no foot sticking up over the tub. The bathtub was empty. There wasn't even any water.

"Hildegarde!" called Mr. Magruder. "Come here."

"Sir?" said the cleaning woman tremulously.

"How do you explain this?"

Hildegarde hesitantly peered into the bathroom. "Why, why . . . he's gone!" she said, clutching her throat.

Mr. Magruder threw open the doors of the closet.

"Gone, and taken his clothes with him."

The cleaning woman collapsed in a chair. "Oh, lordy!" she wailed. "It's the body snatchers."

"Or a ghost!" said Felicity Jones darkly from the doorway.

"A criminal offense, that's what it is—disposing of evidence," said Mr. Lamkin.

Outside in the hallway, Mixed Blessing started a mournful howl.

3

Phillip A. Gusset

Officer Feeney burst into room 107 only to find that the body he had been called upon to investigate had vanished.

"What's this? Some kind of joke?" he asked.

Everyone turned to Hildegarde, and she began to cry.

"I don't know what to say," she wailed. "If the man wasn't dead, he bloody well *should* have been, he looked so awful. You know I don't go around making up stories, Mr. Magruder. Have I ever fibbed to you?"

"I stand behind my cleaning woman," Mr. Magruder said loyally. "Hildegarde has been an honest, faithful employee and never one to create a ruckus."

"Then," said Feeney, "either the man recovered or his body has been spirited away."

"Don't *say* that!" shrieked Mrs. Magruder, who had come to the door of the room.

But Hildegarde just sat on the edge of the bed with her arms wrapped around her and rocked back and forth.

"The body snatchers, they got 'im," she moaned.

"What did you say, Hildegarde?" asked Bernie.

"Them folks what goes about snatching up dead bodies almost before they're cold and selling them to medical schools."

"Nonsense!" said Mrs. Magruder.

"My good people," said Mr. Magruder. "Obviously what we have here is an honest mistake, a sincere misconception, an obscured conclusion. I am sure that Officer Feeney will clear it up in no time, so if you will just go back to your rooms, and if the four Magruder children will return to the apartment forthwith, we shall all get on with enjoying this glorious Saturday."

"To a departed guest," Felicity Jones began reciting as she moved slowly back down the hall, arms crossed over her breast:

> "Though your body has vanished,
> Your clothes and your skin,
> Your spirit resides
> At the Bessledorf Inn."

Back in the apartment, Officer Feeney gathered all the Magruders around the table. Bernie and Joseph looked like their father—brown hair, brown eyes, high foreheads, and large ears. Delores and Lester looked like Mother, with pointy chins and pink cheeks and tiny little ears that looked like the handles of a sugar bowl. No one, however, was smiling.

"Did anyone see the body besides Hildegarde?" Feeney asked. The others shook their heads.

"What was the name of the body in question?"

"Phillip A. Gusset," said Mr. Magruder. "He

checked in yesterday around dinnertime and said he would be leaving this morning."

"A man of his word," said Delores dryly. She did not care to be awakened early on a Saturday morning for nothing.

"Did you notice anything at all unusual about him?" asked Feeney. "Was he sickly? Did his hands shake? Did he glance furtively over his shoulder as though he might be hiding out?"

Mr. Magruder looked around at his brood. "You were all here when Mr. Gusset checked in—the man in the black felt hat with a small red feather on one side. What can you tell Officer Feeney?"

"He had only one bag," offered Bernie. "I carried it down the hall to his room."

"He was very polite," said Delores. "He was coming in just ahead of me, and he held open the door, bowed, and said, 'After you, Mademoiselle.'"

"He had a mustache that hung down like this," said Lester, placing a finger on either side of his mouth.

"The dog didn't like him," said Joseph. "Mixed

Blessing gave him one long, suspicious sniff."

Feeney stuck his notebook back in his pocket. "As far as I can see, there is absolutely nothing here to report," he said. "Man checks in; man leaves in the morning. What Hildegarde says she saw in the bathtub is quite beside the point."

"Then you won't file a report about a murder in the Bessledorf?" asked Mr. Magruder, much relieved.

"The case is dead," said Feeney. "Unless, of course, Mr. Gusset is, in which case the body will turn up sooner or later. Cheerio."

Delores yawned and went back to bed; Joseph went to take a shower; and Lester began pouring a large serving of frosted wheat biscuits into a bowl. But Bernie sat with his head in his hands, thinking it over. Mr. Gusset was the man his parents had been arguing about just that morning, yet neither of them had said anything about it to Officer Feeney.

The policeman kept his word and did not file a report, but by the time Mrs. Buzzwell finished telling the story, it had traveled all through the hotel and down the street to the newspaper office. On Sunday morning, the headline read: "Bessledorf Hotel Guest Mysteriously Disappears," and the reporter went on to quote Mrs. Buzzwell as saying that it was an awful feeling to think that someone may have been murdered right across the hall from her own room.

"Some guests," the story went on, quoting Felicity Jones, "attribute the disappearance to a spiritual debarkation, while others feel that there is foul play afoot in the Bessledorf Hotel."

"We have got to stay calm," said Mrs. Magruder as she paced the floor. "We absolutely must keep our wits about us," she added, her voice rising. And she grabbed her husband by the shoulders. "We cannot afford to be hysterical!" she cried.

"We must act as though nothing out of the ordinary has happened here, and perhaps people will forget it," said Mr. Magruder. "It's a good thing Mr. Fairchild is off in Istanbul. If *he* got wind of this, I might lose my job."

But Bernie, watching from the doorway, wondered what it *really* was about Mr. Gusset—other than cigars and citronella—that had bothered his parents.

That evening, as he was turning out the light in the lobby, he remembered the brown slippers he had seen under Mr. Gusset's bed. Perhaps they had fingerprints on them.

He took the master key from the front desk and crept down the hall to room 107. He would turn the slippers over to Officer Feeney without upsetting his parents further. Then, if Phillip A. Gusset should make news again, the slippers might provide a clue.

Softly he let himself into the room, closed the door behind him, and turned on the light. He crouched down beside the bed and stuck one arm beneath it. His fingers closed around dust balls. Bernie put his cheek against the rug and looked. The slippers were gone.

4

The Bag in the River

On the way to school the next day, Bernie's two closest friends—Wallace ("Weasel") Boyd and Georgene Riley—asked him about the mysterious disappearance.

"It's really spooky, Bernie," Georgene told him, her ponytail swinging. "Nobody will ever want to sleep in that room again."

Weasel pushed up the glasses that kept sliding down his nose. "Yeah, you'll have to change the number on it," he said. "You know the way big hotels don't have a thirteenth floor? They just skip thirteen and call it fourteen instead?"

"That's crazy," said Bernie. "Besides, even if we

did, Mrs. Buzzwell would go across the hall and tell people they were sleeping in a haunted room."

When Bernie got home that afternoon, however, and went down the hall to take Mr. Lamkin his mail, he discovered that the rooms on one side of the hall had been renumbered: 101, 103, 105, 109, and 111.

He was still worrying about those slippers. Officer Feeney had not taken anything from Mr. Gusset's room. Neither had the Magruders. As for Hildegarde, she had declared she would never set foot inside the room again, and it still had not been cleaned; the sheets and towels were lying exactly where Mr. Gusset had left them. The only person Bernie could think of who would have been interested at all in those slippers was Mr. Gusset himself.

He had barely reached the Magruders' apartment when he heard the phone ringing, and Bernie answered. It was Weasel.

"Bernie," he said. "I've been thinking. Whoever stole that body and all its clothes sure got rid of it in a hurry. What's the quickest way you know to get rid of a body?"

Bernie mulled it over. It certainly wouldn't be to bury it. He'd dug a grave for a dog once, and that took long enough. "Throw it in the river, I guess," he said.

"Bingo," said Weasel. "Georgene and I will meet you down at Fletcher's Landing in ten minutes."

When Bernie hung up, he saw Lester watching him from across the kitchen where he was dunking crackers in a cup of chocolate milk.

"Throw what in the river?" Lester asked.

"None of your business," said Bernie and, taking Mixed Blessing with him, hurried out the back door toward Middleburg Park. He followed the creek to the stream and the stream to the river and there, at Fletcher's Landing, were Georgene and Weasel, waiting for him.

"This is the closest the river comes to the Bessledorf Hotel," Weasel said, "so if a body was going to get dumped, I'll bet it would be about here."

"Don't dead men float?" Georgene asked. "Wouldn't we see a body bobbing around out there somewhere?"

Bernie looked out over the water. The river was as quiet and calm as a lake. Here and there a reed rose up out of the water, or a dragonfly skimmed the surface in the late spring sunshine, but there were no lumps, no bulges, no bumps that looked like a body floating on the water. Mixed Blessing prowled happily through the weeds along shore, looking around now and then to make sure the others were coming.

For an hour or more, Bernie and his friends walked along the bank, poking through the marsh grass, sliding on the mud, jabbing down into the water a time or two with sticks.

"If there were a dead body here, Mixed Blessing would have found it by now," said Bernie finally. He was thinking about Mr. Gusset's slippers again. If only he had taken them back to the apartment when he first saw them, he could have given the dog a sniff of them before he left and tracked the body down.

All at once Georgene came to a dead stop, so that Bernie and Weasel bumped into her from behind.

"Look!" she said, one hand over her mouth.

Floating down the river, about five feet out from the bank, was a large plastic bag, secured tightly at both ends with tape.

"I was *right!*" Weasel breathed. "Isn't that the right size for a body?"

The boys pulled off their sneakers and waded out into the cold water until they could pull the bag in with sticks. Bernie felt slightly sick to his stomach. What would a body look like that had been floating on the river for three days? There was a small hump at one end where the head would be, one at the other where the feet would go, and a large round lump in the middle for the stomach. Mixed Blessing had waded out into the water beside them and stood with his tail stiff, nose thrust forward, sniffing.

"Maybe we ought to go get Officer Feeney," Georgene said, helping to pull the bag over.

"No, we'll open it first," said Bernie, holding onto his end. He hoped he had the end with the feet.

"Who wants to go first?" asked Weasel, and this time his voice trembled just a little.

"Why don't you both open the bag together?" Georgene suggested. "Ready, set, go. . . ."

Bernie and Weasel unwound the tape. Slowly, Bernie peeked in the bag. There was a shoe, all right. Then another and another. He opened the bag wider. Out fell an old boot, a pizza wrapper, a torn bath towel, a grapefruit peel, a chicken carcass, a bunch of old magazines, and a Cheerios box. From the look on Weasel's face, there was more of the same at his end.

"It's just garbage!" said Weasel. And then, from up the bank, came a loud giggle, followed by a laugh.

"Lester!" said Bernie, as his brother streaked through the trees and made a beeline back toward Middleburg Park. "He emptied all the wastebaskets there in the hotel and dumped them here in the river just to trick us."

Mixed Blessing grabbed the chicken carcass in his mouth and took off after Lester.

Bernie disgustedly closed the bag up again and dragged it to a trash container back in the park.

"Too bad it wasn't Lester who disappeared," said Weasel. "Maybe if you put him in that room overnight, *he'd* be gone the next morning."

"Well, anyway, we tried," said Georgene. "We checked the river, and I'll bet that's more than the police have done."

But Bernie was terribly disappointed. It would have been great to see their names in the paper. "Bernie and Friends Find Body," the headline might even have said. All he had waiting for him now back at the hotel was Lester.

5

C·O·M·B·O

That evening, Theodore Magruder went off to sing in his barbershop quartet and left Joseph in charge of the front desk. Salt Water was pacing back and forth on the counter. "Zip your lip, zip your lip," the parrot squawked, and pecked at paper clips as Bernie cleaned up under his perch. The phone rang.

"Bessledorf Hotel," Joseph said into the receiver.

Even from where he stood, Bernie could hear Mr. Fairchild's voice at the other end of the line. Robert L. Fairchild was the owner of the hotel. He lived in Indianapolis, and whenever something was wrong, he called. When something was *really* wrong, he flew down to Middleburg and arrived unannounced.

"What in thunder is going on in my hotel?" he roared. "I just got in this evening and took a look at the newspaper."

Joseph winced and held the receiver out away from his ear.

"What . . . what do you mean, sir?" he said.

"What I mean is where is the guest that disappeared so mysteriously from my hotel that the story is on page three of the Indianapolis paper?"

"I wish I knew, sir," said Joseph. "The police investigated and concluded that the body just up and left, and they didn't even file a report. But somehow the newspaper got hold of the story."

"When a body gets up and walks out, that's news!" said Mr. Fairchild. "Listen, Joseph, you tell your father I don't want any more of this foolishness; it's not good for business. And furthermore, you tell him that beginning Friday night, I want live entertainment in the hotel dining room on weekends to bring the customers back. You tell him that I want a combo."

"A combo, sir!" exclaimed Joseph.

"Combo!" said Mr. Fairchild. "C as in clarinet, O as in oboe, M as in marimba, B as in bass, and O as in out-on-the-street, where the Magruders will be if business drops off at the Bessledorf."

"How much will you pay a combo, Mr. Fairchild?"

"I won't pay them anything at all!" roared the owner. "I wasn't responsible for a body disappearing out from under my very nose. Your father can pay for it out of his own salary or he can find some musicians who are willing to play for free. But I want a combo there by Friday night."

"What are we going to do, Joseph?" Bernie asked after Mr. Fairchild hung up. No matter how difficult things were, Bernie had faith in Joseph because he went to college. Anyone who was studying animals ought to know something about live entertainment.

"We'll think of something," said Joseph, "but don't tell Mother. She'll only worry."

Georgene and Weasel came over with their skateboards, and Bernie went with them to Bessledorf Hill, just as the moon was beginning to show in the sky. But Bernie didn't feel like riding. He tried but fell off before he even got down as far as the parachute factory.

"What's wrong, Bernie?" asked Weasel, pushing his glasses up on his nose again. "You won't get in *The Guinness Book of World Records* this way. You won't even come close."

Bernie told them about the live combo the Magruders had to have by Friday night.

"Let's look some up in the want ads," said Georgene. "Musicians always advertise in the want ads."

They went to the bus depot and found an old newspaper lying on a bench. Weasel turned to the want ads.

"For hire," he read. "Magicians . . . mechanics . . . morticians . . . musicians . . . Here we go." He spread the newspaper out on the bench.

Rock band: "The Elastic Ambassadors."

Three hours of entertainment, $175.

Bernie gulped. They looked some more.

Jazz combo: "The Missing Links."

Singer and four musicians, $325.

Bernie choked. "We could never afford that," he said.

Slowly they walked back to the hotel lobby.

"You could always put on a record," Georgene suggested helpfully. "Have your sister stand at the microphone in a long dress and move her lips. Maybe that would do it."

"We'll think of something," said Bernie. "Joseph always does." He walked inside and his friends went home.

But Joseph hadn't thought of anything yet except how it would feel to be kicked out onto the sidewalk. Mr. Fairchild meant what he said: The Magruders could manage his hotel only as long as business was good. Two other managers had lost their jobs before Mr. Magruder, and there were plenty of people who were ready to take over at a moment's notice. Jobs were hard to find in Middleburg.

Nine-year-old Lester walked through the lobby eating a peanut-butter-potato-chip sandwich. Little globs of peanut butter stuck to the corners of his mouth. Every time he took a bite, potato chip crumbs rained down on his T-shirt. Bernie tried not to watch.

"What's the matter?" asked Lester, looking first at Joseph, then at Bernie.

"Nothing," said Bernie. "Just thinking what it would be like to live at the bus station."

Lester stopped chewing. "We going to move again, Joseph?" he asked, his eyes wide.

"No," said Joseph, "not if we can come up with a live combo crazy enough to play for free in a hotel where a body has mysteriously disappeared."

Lester licked his fingers one at a time. "Dad's been sacked," he guessed.

"No, he hasn't," said Bernie. "Not yet, anyway. But don't say a word to Mom. Joseph will think of something."

At that moment a cab pulled up to the front

entrance and a woman got out. She came inside, stepped over Mixed Blessing there on the mat, set her suitcase down, and walked up to the desk.

Her hair was orange, her glasses were tinted green, her lips and cheeks were rouged red, and around her neck she wore a blue feather boa, which dangled down onto her arms.

"I need a room," she said, "and I want it as far away from the dead man's room as I can get."

"I'm afraid I don't understand, ma'am," said Joseph, playing dumb.

"You know good and well what I'm talking about," the woman said. "It's been in all the papers. I want to get as far away from room 107 as I can."

Joseph opened the guest register. "This hotel has no record of any deaths, ma'am," he said politely, "but if you wish to be far away from room 107, I can give you a room on the third floor."

"Is it near a fire escape?" asked the woman. "I am deathly afraid of fires."

"I can give you a room with a fire escape right outside your window," said Joseph.

So the lady wrote down her name, Ethel King, and Bernie carried her suitcase up to room 321. As they went up on the elevator, he realized that Mr. Fairchild was right. The lady with the orange hair and green glasses had already heard about the mysterious disappearance. She probably wouldn't stay at the hotel very long, and there were others who wouldn't stay at the Bessledorf at all. A combo would help.

The woman gave Bernie a package of gum as a tip, and Bernie went back down just as his father came home.

Mr. Magruder was standing at the desk listening intently as Joseph told him about the phone call from Mr. Fairchild. Bernie watched his father's face. Would they pack up and leave? Or would Father have to pay half a week's salary to hire some musicians?

"No problem," said Father, beginning to smile. "No problem at all. If Fairchild wants live entertainment, that's what he'll get. Beginning Friday evening, the Red Bananas will be performing on weekends in the Bessledorf dining room."

"The Red Bananas?" asked Joseph.

"My barbershop quartet," said Father.

6

The Red Bananas

A large banner went up outside the Bessledorf Hotel the following day:

THE RED BANANAS NOW APPEARING
WEEKENDS AT THE BESSLEDORF
BARBERSHOP SINGING AT ITS FINEST

Wilbur Wilkins, the handyman, hung it just above the hotel canopy.

"Can't figure why anyone would want to come and listen to a bunch of fruit," he muttered through his mustache, but he built a small stage at one end of the dining room and helped set up the microphone.

"Theodore, what is all this?" Mrs. Magruder asked. "The cook is upset and the waiters want to know how they're supposed to serve dinner without blocking the view of the stage."

"We will all have to manage the best we can," her husband told her. "If Mrs. Verona can't cook to music, then she'll have to pack up her strudel and go somewhere else."

"Theodore!" gasped mother.

"I'm sorry, my dear, but I have a lot on my mind," Mr. Magruder said. "Do forgive me. Music will be good for business, so please don't worry your head about it."

"But your quartet has never performed in public!" said his wife.

"Well, then it's time we did," said Mr. Magruder. "We haven't been practicing every Monday night for the past six months for nothing."

Friday night came, and all the Magruder children were on hand to help out. Joseph took over the front desk so that his father could sing; Delores offered to do the announcing; Lester handed out programs at the door, and Bernie sat behind the stage curtain controlling the lights and microphone.

Peeping out around the curtain, he saw Georgene Riley and Weasel come in and take a table near the door. They ordered chocolate sundaes just so they could hear the music.

Mr. Fairchild had the right idea, Bernie was thinking, because every time a bus stopped out front, more people got off and came inside the hotel. Live music at dinner was quite a novelty in Middleburg, and it wasn't every day that people got to hear a group called the Red Bananas. Mrs. Magruder, smiling, led them all to tables and offered them menus, until every seat was taken and a line formed in the lobby.

At eight o'clock, Theodore Magruder's quartet walked into the dining room to polite applause. There was a tiny little man who sang bass, a giant of a man who sang tenor, a round, fat man who sang baritone, and Theodore himself, who sang the melody. They all wore white jackets and navy trousers and bright red ties, with red bands around their straw hats.

Bernie clicked on the microphone, dimmed the

lights, and turned the spotlight on the stage. Delores got up and told the audience that the Bessledorf was the first hotel in Middleburg to offer live performers on weekends.

"And *dead* folks in between," called out someone from the audience.

People snickered, and Delores's face flushed. But she soon got control of herself and went on:

"And now," she said, "the Bessledorf Hotel takes great pleasure in presenting the Red Bananas, who will start off with three old favorites: 'Sweet Adeline,' 'Kentucky Babe,' and 'Lida Rose.'" Delores made a little curtsey and went back to her seat. The quartet moved into the spotlight. The round, fat man blew a note on his pitch pipe, and the others hummed their notes softly, then grew quiet.

Theodore Magruder leaned toward the microphone and began singing in his clear, ringing voice: "Sweet Adeline . . ." and the other three men put their heads together and crooned, "Sweet . . . A . . . de . . . line."

Bernie was pleasantly surprised. They didn't

sound half bad. At the end of the first song the big giant of a man let his voice go higher and higher, and the tiny little man let his deep bass voice go lower and lower until the audience broke in with hearty applause.

Mrs. Verona, the cook, had baked special sugar cakes for dessert, which appeared on the menu as "Sweet Adelines," and everyone ordered some with coffee. More chairs were set up along the walls for the people waiting outside, and at the end of the evening the kitchen had sold out of everything and the quartet did an encore.

When the dining room closed at last, Bernie went out to the lobby where Felicity Jones, Mr. Lamkin, and Mrs. Buzzwell had started a game of cards. He found Georgene and Weasel over by the Coke machine.

"Who called out that remark about dead folks during the week?" he whispered.

"It was a woman," said Weasel. "She had orange hair and green glasses and red lips and blue feathers around her neck."

"Ethel King, in room 321!" said Bernie. "I wonder why she even bothered to come?"

The Bessledorf was in a good mood that night, however. Waiters whistled as they vacuumed the rug and put the chairs up on the tables. Mrs. Verona sang as she chopped vegetables for the next day. Mr. Magruder hummed to himself as he counted out the day's receipts, and Bernie felt sure that the worst was over.

At ten o'clock, the waiters carried the "goodnight specials" around to all the guests in their rooms. Every night, each guest got his choice of coffee, tea, or cocoa before bedtime.

Bernie went out in the kitchen to help Mrs. Verona put the beverages on a serving cart. First the coffees went around, then the teas, and then the waiters came back for the cocoas.

At that moment there was the sound of hurried feet crossing the lobby, then the dining room, and finally the door to the kitchen flew open. One of the waiters staggered in and collapsed in a chair. Felicity Jones, Mrs. Buzzwell, and Mr. Lamkin, following along behind, peeped curiously around the corner.

"Hopkins!" cried Mrs. Verona. "What's wrong with you?"

The waiter was a rather large boy of seventeen with a round face, and at that particular moment it was the color of a bleached dish towel. Mrs. Verona began fanning him with her apron.

"Hopkins!" she said again. "What happened?"

"I didn't do it," he gasped. "I swear I didn't."

"Do what?" asked Bernie, unbuttoning the boy's collar.

"Kill her," said Hopkins.

Mrs. Verona stopped fanning. "Kill *whom*?"

"The door was open," the waiter gulped. "I couldn't help but see her feet, and there she was—sprawled right out on the floor."

"*Who,* you exasperating boy?" cried Mrs. Verona, whopping him with her apron.

"The woman in 321," said Hopkins. "Dead as a doornail."

7

Ethel King

They all stood around Hopkins, who had a cold wet towel on his forehead and sick look about the mouth. Mrs. Verona went rushing around the kitchen turning all the pots and kettles upside down so that if the dead woman's spirit happened to wander through, it would not settle in one of her saucepans.

Mr. Magruder hurried into the kitchen when he heard about it. "Who was it?" he asked quickly.

"The woman in 321, sir," gasped Hopkins, his chin quivering.

Father grabbed Bernie by one arm and Hopkins

by the other. "We'll check this out," he said, starting for the lobby.

"Theodore," said Mother, weeping, "what on earth will we tell Mr. Fairchild when he hears about this?"

Mr. Magruder shook his head. "Alma, my dear, make no phone calls to the police until we get back."

As they started up the stairs, Father turned to the round-faced waiter once more. "Are you sure she was dead?" he asked. "Was she breathing?"

"Oh, Mr. Magruder, sir, I didn't stop to check," the waiter said, wiping the sweat from his forehead.

"What do you figure this is all about, Dad?" Bernie asked.

"I don't know," said his father, "but this time I'm keeping quiet. *Nobody's* going to know until . . ."

He stopped as they opened the stairwell door at third, for there stood Felicity Jones outside room 321, holding a rose in her hand. Mrs. Buzzwell and Mr. Lamkin were there, too.

"We overheard Hopkins in the kitchen," Felicity Jones said, "and I just had to compose a song for the funeral:

OH, FAIREST LADY, HAIR OF ORANGE

THAT EVER WINDS DIDST BLOW,

THE ZEPHYRS WEEP BUT FOLLOW STILL

WHEREVER THOU DOST GO."

"Felicity, my dear," said Mr. Magruder, "why don't you go back to your room and write a sonnet about

A YOUNG WOMAN NAMED JONES,

WHO SEEMED TO HAVE DELICATE BONES.

THEY PUT HER TO BED,

BUT BY MORNING HER HEAD

HAD FILLED UP COMPLETELY WITH STONES."

"Why, Mr. Magruder," said Felicity, "I had no idea you were a poet!" And she trailed off down the hall, sniffing the rose and sighing loudly.

But Mr. Lamkin and Mrs. Buzzwell would not move.

"We *demand* to know what is going on in this hotel," said Mrs. Buzzwell.

Mr. Magruder pushed opened the door to room 321, which Hopkins had left ajar, and slowly looked inside.

"What do you see, Dad? Is she dead?" Bernie asked, trying to look in under his father's arm.

Mr. Magruder opened the door wider. "See for yourself, Bernie. She's gone."

Bernie started at the floor where the woman with the orange hair was supposed to be lying. Bare as a baby's bottom.

They went into the room and even peeped in the bathtub, just to make sure. Empty. The drawers were empty, the closets empty, nothing in or under the bed. But the window to the fire escape was open.

Bernie walked over and looked out. There was no sign at all of the woman with the orange hair, green glasses, ruby red cheeks, and the blue feathers round her neck. Goose bumps rose up on his arms.

"Theodore?" came Mother's cautious voice from the doorway. "Where is the body?"

"Gone," said Mr. Magruder.

"What? Oh, Theodore, not again!"

"Better no body at all than a body with a bullet in the head," said Mr. Magruder. "Whoever is dying on us at least has the consideration to pick themselves up afterward and walk away."

"Maybe she just fainted," said Bernie, trying to figure it out.

"Fainted on purpose, I'm thinking," said his father. "She must have timed it so that when the good-night specials were delivered, she'd be found there on the rug."

Mrs. Magruder timidly came into the room and looked about. She lifted her head and sniffed, then went to the window and sniffed some more.

"Theodore," she said finally, "does this room remind you of anything?"

"As a matter of fact it does," said Mr. Magruder. "Old sweat socks and a pastrami on rye."

"Oh, no!" said Mother, leaning her hands on

the windowsill and looking out. "Heliotrope and a full moon and a porch swing going *squeakity squank, squeakity squank.*"

"I wish I knew what was going on between you two," said Bernie to his parents.

"I can't explain it anymore than your father can," said Mother. "It's just a scent, a wisp of a scent, I think, that seems to upset your father, but not me."

"Since there's no body, we might as well go back downstairs," said Mr. Magruder, closing the window to the fire escape and locking it.

When they got to the lobby, Officer Feeney was waiting. So were Mr. Lamkin and Mrs. Buzzwell.

"Okay, Magruder, what's the idea of a cover-up?" Feeney asked.

"A what?"

"You know. Another body disappears, and do I get a call? Does the hotel manager bother to call the police? The phone rings at headquarters, and Mr. Lamkin here fills me in. Second time in a row, Theodore, that I've arrived to find the body gone."

"I'm as puzzled as you are, Feeney," said Bernie's father. "If I had any idea where the woman went, I'd go after her myself, especially since she hasn't paid her bill."

"Well, I can't very well report a dead body if it got up and walked away. Might have been a woman doing her exercises. Just 'cause a woman's flat on her back on the floor don't mean she's passed on."

"Oh, thank goodness," said Mother. "I was so afraid you'd file a report."

"But what I *am* suspectin', ma'am, to tell the truth, is that someone around here thinks Feeney hasn't got enough to do and is pullin' his leg. The next time I get a report of a body at the Bessledorf, it better be a dead one."

"We'll see what we can do," said Mr. Magruder.

"I can feel it coming," murmured Mrs. Buzzwell. "One evening you'll bring the good-night special to my room, and there I'll be on the floor, dead as a mackerel. We'll all go, one by one."

"A foreign plot, mark my words," said Mr. Lamkin.

"My good people, you have overactive imaginations," said Mr. Magruder. "Tomorrow is another day—a beautiful day, I understand—and the sooner you get to bed, the sooner you can get up and enjoy yourselves."

Mr. Lamkin and Mrs. Buzzwell retired, leaving Bernie and his parents to lock up. The cats watched from the window seat, Salt Water nodded on his perch, and Mixed Blessing put his head on his paws as though it were just another peaceful night at the Bessledorf, but Bernie knew better.

He watched anxiously as his father went about the lobby checking the locks on all the doors and windows. What if the body snatchers weren't outside the hotel but were already inside? That's what worried Bernie.

As Mrs. Magruder pulled the drapes, she looked out once more and whispered, "Heliotrope."

8

The Bus to Muncie

"Poet Composes; Body Disposed of," was the banner headline in the newspaper the next morning.

"How on earth did the reporters find out about this?" Mrs. Magruder gasped when she opened her paper.

"Mrs. Buzzwell, you can bet," said Delores, stuffing a piece of toast in her mouth. "She can probably hear me chewing this very minute. I can just see it now, Mother. Everyone will be talking about us, no one will ever come to this hotel again, I'll never meet any men my own age, and I will go on working at the parachute factory for the rest of my natural life."

"Nonsense," said Mother. "There's nothing that makes a young man more protective of a woman than to feel that he is rescuing her from her own family."

"If this story made the Indianapolis papers," said Father darkly, "we'll have a lot more to worry about than that. If Mr. Fairchild has read the paper, any minute our phone will ring, and—"

The phone rang. Mr. Magruder looked at his wife and Mrs. Magruder looked at Joseph and Joseph looked at Delores, but it was Bernie who answered.

"Which Magruder is this?" boomed Mr. Fairchild on the other end.

"Bernie, sir."

"What's this about another body disappearing from my hotel? What are you folks doing down there—shipping them out on a conveyor belt?"

"Well, sir, she was here one minute and gone the next," Bernie said, trying to explain, at which point his father took over the phone.

"Listen, Mr. Fairchild," he said, "we are doing

the very best we can. You wanted entertainment, you got entertainment, and the Bessledorf dining room did its best business yet. Give us a chance, and I'm sure things will turn out all right."

Bernie had never heard his father talk quite that way to Mr. Fairchild and silently cheered him on. Mr. Magruder held the receiver out away from his ear for whatever Mr. Fairchild would say next, but instead of yelling, the hotel owner sounded a little subdued.

"Well," he said, "you got your combo lined up again for tonight? The Pink Pineapples or whatever it was?"

"The Red Bananas," Mr. Magruder told him. "Yes, sir, we are all set to go."

"All right then, Magruder," Fairchild said, his voice booming again, "but I'm keeping an eye on you. I've got a good hotel down there, and I want to keep it in business. You understand?"

"Perfectly," said Mr. Magruder.

When he hung up, Joseph said, "Bad news, Dad. I just tallied up what the woman with the orange

56

hair owed us. Ethel King slipped away with a bill of $68.17, not counting her dinner last night."

Mrs. Magruder moaned.

Lester, who was noisily eating a bowl of cornflakes, wiped the sleeve of his bathrobe across his mouth.

"Know what we ought to do, Dad?" he grunted. "Put bars on all the windows so nobody can get out."

"Eat your cornflakes, Lester," said his father glumly.

"Well, it could be that Ethel King hasn't left Middleburg yet," said Bernie. "I'm going to get Georgene and Weasel and look around the bus depot. If we find her, we'll ask Officer Feeney to make an arrest."

"Good thinking!" said Mr. Magruder, brightening. "Good thinking, indeed!"

Within ten minutes, Georgene Riley and Weasel were at the bus depot next door to the Bessledorf Hotel, walking among the benches, peering at faces over by the ticket counter, looking for the woman with the orange hair.

"I *thought* she was a phony," said Georgene. "Her hair looked like something that grew on a tree in Florida."

"And those blue feathers!" said Weasel. "They looked like they came from a polyester pigeon."

"So what were we supposed to do?" Bernie asked. "Tell her she couldn't stay in our hotel because she looked funny?"

"Bus now leaving for Anderson, Muncie, Huntington, and Fort Wayne," said a voice on the loudspeaker. "Gate seven."

People stood up and began gathering together their suitcases and bags.

"Hey! " said Bernie. "Isn't that the woman with the orange hair?"

At the far end of the depot, an orange head was moving along with the crowd toward gate seven.

"Go get Officer Feeney!" Bernie told Weasel, and then, to Georgene, "Somehow you've got to distract her before she gets past the gate. I'm going to try to get up to the ticket man and head her off."

"*How* am I suppose to distract her, for heaven's sake?" Georgene wanted to know.

"You'll think of something," Bernie said confidently and began edging his way through the crowd toward the gate man who was checking tickets.

On up ahead, the orange head got closer and closer to the door. Suddenly a loud wail filled the bus depot, and people stopped and turned around. There stood Georgene Riley, wiping her eyes, crying pitifully.

"Waaaah!" wailed Georgene again. "My aunt's going to Muncie, and I didn't get a chance to kiss her good-bye."

Good grief, thought Bernie.

"Where is your aunt, dear?" asked a kind man.

"That woman up there with the orange hair," sobbed Georgene convincingly. "Aunt Gladys. All I want to do is hug her one last time."

The kind man tapped the shoulder of the woman in front of him and she tapped the shoulder of the man in front of her and on it went, right up the line. And all the while Bernie was working himself closer and closer to the ticket man at the gate. Just as the orange head reached the ticket man, someone tapped her on the shoulder and she turned around.

Bernie gulped. It was not orange hair at all. It was a fuzzy angora cap, and it rested on the head of a dark-haired woman with wire-rimmed glasses.

"Why, bless my stars," said the woman in the orange cap when she heard the story, "but I don't have a niece in the world. Tell the little girl she's got the wrong auntie." And the woman in the orange cap went on through the gate and boarded the bus to Muncie.

At that moment Officer Feeney and Weasel came hurrying through the depot.

"Where is she?" called Weasel. "I've got Officer Feeney. He's going to arrest her for trying to skip town without paying her bill."

Bernie made his way back through the crowd.

"Mistake," he mumbled. "It wasn't her, Weasel. I'm afraid Ethel King's given us the slip."

"Wasn't *her!*" shrieked Georgene. "You mean I stood here bawling for nothing?"

"You sent me chasing all over town for Feeney, and it wasn't even her?" hollered Weasel.

Officer Feeney patted his nightstick against the palm of his other hand. "You know what I'm thinking?" he said dryly. "I'm thinking that maybe the Bessledorf would be a better place if the whole Magruder clan just packed their bags and moved to Maine."

He turned and left the depot, and Bernie walked silently back to the hotel, Georgene and Weasel following some distance behind. They were still friends, he knew; they wouldn't give up on him that easily. But oh, it would have been something if the woman *had* been Ethel King and Feeney had made a grand arrest right there in the bus station.

9

What Happened to Charlie

Bernie didn't have time to worry anymore about Ethel King's vanishing act, however, because the hotel was getting ready for the second night of the Red Bananas. He was passing through the apartment kitchen around two when the phone rang.

"Hello?" he said, but there was no response from the other end.

"Hello?" Bernie said again, louder. This time he thought he heard something—a raspy cheep, perhaps—but finally he hung up. He did not think about it again until four, when he went by the front desk in the lobby and the phone rang again, as it had all afternoon. Everyone wanted reservations for the night's performance. Joseph answered:

"Bessledorf Hotel. Thirty rooms, reasonably priced, with live entertainment on Friday and Saturday nights. May I help you?"

There was a pause.

"Bessledorf Hotel," Joseph said again, louder.

Bernie stopped, wondering.

Joseph held the receiver out away from his ear and said to Bernie, "There's someone on the line. I can hear him breathing, but he won't answer."

Goose bumps rose up on Bernie's arms. The first thing he thought of was Mr. Gusset. Mr. Gusset's ghost, perhaps. Or was it Ethel King, pulling another trick?

"Bessledorf Hotel," Joseph said the third time, and when there was still no answer, he hung up.

The more Bernie thought about it, the more he began to worry about the brown slippers he had seen under Mr. Gusset's bed. When Georgene and Weasel came by about three, he told them about the slippers.

"Why didn't you tell your father?" Weasel asked.

Bernie shook his head. "I don't know. There's something about Mr. Gusset and Ethel King both that upsets my parents. When Phillip Gusset checked in, Mother said he reminded her of heliotrope, but Dad said that Gusset reminded him of cigars. When they were in Ethel King's room after she disappeared, Mom said the room reminded her of porch swings and full moons, and Dad said it reminded him of old sweat socks."

Weasel looked at Bernie. "You've sure got weird parents," he said.

Bernie turned helplessly to Georgene. "I just can't bring myself to tell them that the slippers walked off by themselves after everything else that's happened."

Georgene nodded understandingly. "That would push them off the deep end, all right," she agreed.

"What I'm afraid of," Bernie told her, "is that someone's going to cause trouble tonight. Maybe

Ethel King will come back and call out insults to the singers."

Georgene flexed her arm muscle. "We'll be your bouncers, Bernie. One word out of Ethel King or anyone else, and we'll escort them to the door."

It was good to have friends he could trust, Bernie thought that evening as he put on his best trousers and shirt. All the Magruders were excited about the big crowd that was expected, and the tables were all taken for the eight o'clock performance.

People began arriving as early as six-thirty. Mrs. Magruder moved back and forth between the dining room and hotel kitchen, seeing that everything was going all right, while Joseph manned the front desk and Mr. Magruder greeted dinner guests in the lobby. Lester had taken Mixed Blessing and the cats to the cellar so that they would not bother anyone, and only Salt Water was left on his perch in the lobby.

"Shake a leg, shake a leg," he admonished ladies as they came in. They stopped and stared at him.

"Hello, Jack! Hello, Jack!" he said to the men.

At seven-fifteen, the phone rang at the front desk, and Bernie answered for Joseph, who was registering a hotel guest.

"Bessledorf Hotel," said Bernie.

Again there was nothing on the line but the strange raspy breathing and now and then what sounded like a frog.

"Listen," said Bernie, "I don't know who you are, but we are very busy tonight and don't have time for jokes." He hung up.

The dining room was packed. Mr. Magruder went up onstage briefly to make an announcement. He said that due to the huge crowd, the Red Bananas would perform twice that evening, once at eight and again at nine-thirty. He said he hoped that those watching the first show would be courteous enough to leave when it was over so that a second crowd could be seated. He looked splendid indeed in his white jacket and navy blue trousers and red tie. No matter how many bodies disappeared at the Bessledorf, Bernie thought, his father would keep the hotel going.

At five minutes of eight, the tiny little man who sang bass arrived, then the round, fat man who sang baritone, but there was no sign of the big giant of a man who sang tenor.

"Oh, no!" said Mr. Magruder. "What's happened to Charlie?"

At that moment, Charlie walked in.

"We were worried," scolded Mr. Magruder. "We were afraid something might have happened."

Charlie opened his mouth, but nothing came out. He pointed to his throat and moved his lips, but he couldn't make a sound. Finally he took a pad and pencil from his pocket and scribbled something down.

"Laryngitis," the note said.

10

Cream on the Side

Bernie's father stared at Charlie. "I don't believe this," he said.

Charlie took his pen again and wrote another message: *I tried to call you, but couldn't speak. Kept hoping that maybe, by tonight, I'd have my voice back.*

Mr. Magruder grabbed his arm and pulled him into the coatroom. "Charlie, are you telling me that my dining room is packed, and the Red Bananas can't go on?"

Charlie tried desperately to say something. The veins on his neck stood out and his face grew red with effort. His lips formed the words, *I'm sorry.*

Delores came to the door of the coatroom. "Time to go on," she said. "Are you ready?"

Mr. Magruder turned to Charlie. "The show must go on. We are all going up on that stage together, and the least you can do is mouth the words. Maybe the audience won't know the difference."

Bernie felt his heart sink.

"But . . . ," protested the little bass and the round, fat baritone together.

"Can you think of a better idea?" asked Mr. Magruder.

The bass and baritone shook their heads.

"Then on with the show," said Mr. Magruder.

The four men put on their straw hats with the red bands, and Bernie went back behind the stage curtain and dimmed the house lights.

Waiters scurried around trying to collect the dinner plates before the program began. Forks clattered and glasses clinked. As the dishes were removed, another waiter wheeled the dessert cart around, placing chocolate tarts in front of all the diners and a big bowl of whipped cream in the center of each table. A third waiter filled the coffee cups.

People began turning their chairs toward the stage. The clatter and chatter grew dimmer until finally there was only the sound of whisperings and the soft whir of the wheels of the dessert cart.

Bernie turned on the spotlight. Delores, in her pretty blue dress, stepped up onstage.

"Good evening, ladies and gentlemen," she said. "The Bessledorf is pleased to present, for the second time, the famous barbershop quartet. . . ."

Bernie covered his face with his hands.

". . . the Red Bananas! Let's give them a big welcome!" Delores started clapping and the audience joined in.

One by one, the four members of the Red Bananas took their places in the spotlight as Delores sat back down. Charlie looked scared or sick or both. The round, fat man blew a note on his pitch pipe and the others, Charlie excluded, hummed their notes. Then Mr. Magruder stepped toward the microphone and his mellow voice filled the dining room:

"Skeeters are a-hummin' on the honeysuckle vine. . . ."

The other three men put their heads together: "Sleep, Kentucky . . . Babe. . . ."

There was something not quite right, Bernie could tell. The voices were in tune, the words distinct, the melody clear, but something—namely, Charlie's voice—was missing.

Theodore sang the next line and then the others chimed in again with "Sleep, Kentucky . . . Babe. . . ."

There was a strange pause. This time, on the word "Babe," Bernie remembered, the tenor was supposed to slide down from one note to another while the other voices held. The tenor did not slide; his voice was not there.

Bernie peeped out from behind the curtain. People in the audience were looking at each other, eyebrows raised. As the men sang on, Bernie changed the spotlight from red to blue, but it didn't help. Couples leaned over tables, whispering to each other and frowning.

Beads of sweat began to form on Charlie's face. And finally, when the quartet reached the chorus, he made a valiant effort to find his voice:

"Fl . . . y, away," the men sang, and it sounded as though someone had let a bullfrog into the dining room. People started to laugh. As Charlie croaked on, the whispers turned to murmurs and the laughter turned to howls.

Splatt!

Bernie thought he saw it coming, a white streak in the air, but before he could blink, it landed on the tenor's shoulder: whipped cream.

Someone hooted in derision. The quartet tried desperately to continue, but Bernie could see someone standing up at the back of the room holding a big glob of whipped cream on a fork. Taking aim, he bent the fork back and again let the cream fly, but this time it landed on the bald head of a man in the front row.

The bald-headed customer lurched to his feet, looking angrily about, then picked up the bowl of whipped cream in the center of his table and threw it, bowl and all, toward the man in the back of the room. It landed in the lap of a lady.

"Now just a minute!" yelled the man who was sitting with the lady, who was staring in astonishment at the whipped cream in her lap.

Whup! Another bowl went flying through the air, and the dining room was in an uproar. The quartet left the stage, some going one way, some another. Mr. Magruder grabbed the microphone and tried to maintain order, but already people were starting to leave. Others grabbed their own bowls of whipped cream and heaved them about the room.

Bernie turned on the house lights just as Officer Feeney appeared in the doorway, Georgene on one side of him, Weasel on the other.

The dining room grew very quiet. People began gathering up their coats and purses and moving toward the door. In a matter of minutes the room was empty except for the waiters, the cook, the quartet, the Magruders, and the whipped cream.

"Fifteen years on the force," said Feeney, "and I

get assigned to this hotel. I could have been on homicide, the vice squad, or the SWAT team, and what do I get? The lunatic fringe. Whipped cream all over the floor. Somebody's out to do you in, Magruder, and we better find him before the Bessledorf goes under."

11

The News Hits the Fan

"Charlie," said Bernie's father, turning to the big giant of a man who sang, or didn't sing, tenor. "I owe you an apology. I had no business asking you to go up on that stage. I should have known what might happen. Do forgive me."

Charlie ran one finger through the whipped cream on his shoulder and licked it off. He nodded to show Mr. Magruder that he accepted his apology.

Lester came up out of the basement where he had been pet-sitting Mixed Blessing and the cats. "You had a food fight and you didn't invite me!" he cried, when he saw the whipped cream on the floor. "You get all the fun!" The cats, Lewis and Clark, were already lapping up the cream.

"Have a tart, Lester," Father said, handing him one from off a table.

While Mr. Magruder walked his quartet to the door, Bernie and Georgene and Weasel sat down in the lobby beside Salt Water's perch. The parrot fluttered down into Bernie's lap and sat with his head erect, his eyes unmoving.

"Who started it?" Bernie asked his friends.

"The whipped-cream throwing? A man, one I never saw before," said Georgene.

"Right after he threw it, he left," said Weasel.

"Why didn't you follow him?"

"Because when the bald-headed man up front started throwing back, I figured I'd better stick around in case you needed me," said Weasel. "When *everyone* started to throw, that's when Georgene and I ran outside to get Feeney."

"Do you remember what the man looked like?" Bernie asked. "I could barely make him out." He was not at all sure it wasn't Phillip Gusset coming back to start a new round of trouble.

"He was sort of average height, not too fat, not too thin, with thick glasses and a big nose," Georgene remembered.

"No mustache that hung down at the corners?" Bernie asked.

Georgene shook her head. "But I'd recognize him if I saw him again, I'm sure."

"Tomorrow, then," said Bernie. "We'll go up and down every street in Middleburg, see if we can spot him. Bring your skateboards so we can really make time."

It was a somber Sunday the following morning. Just as Mr. Magruder feared, there was a story on the first page of the *Middleburg Post:*

"Bananas Split" the headline read, and below, "Quartet Attacked by Whipped Cream; Melee Follows."

The six Magruders sat listlessly around the breakfast table, their eyes on the telephone.

"Any minute now, Mr. Fairchild is going to read the story in the Indianapolis paper," said Mr.

Magruder. "They always send stories like this out over the wire services so that every paper in the country can pick it up."

"He'll be sitting down to breakfast right about now," said Mrs. Magruder. "His wife will hand him the orange juice, then the toast, and finally the paper. . . ."

"Then he'll unfold it and start to choke," said Delores.

"Why don't we all just go on a picnic?" Lester said brightly, mashing a banana with his fork and pouring syrup on it. "Then, if the phone rings, we won't be here to answer."

"Eat your banana, Lester," said his father.

The phone rang. Everyone jumped. Mrs. Magruder was so nervous she spilled her coffee.

"I'll get it," said Joseph. "You've both been through enough. Let me handle it this time." He reached for the phone on the wall behind him.

"Bessledorf Hotel," he said, and then held out the receiver so he wouldn't go deaf. It was Mr. Fairchild, all right.

"What in thunder have I got down there?" Mr. Fairchild bellowed, and his voice boomed out over the whole kitchen. "A magic show, with disappearing bodies? A dairy store? What am I paying you Magruders for—to throw whipped cream around and get my hotel in the papers every Sunday?"

"It was an act of nature, Mr. Fairchild," Joseph told him. "The tenor had laryngitis and couldn't sing his part. Someone in the audience showed his displeasure by throwing his dessert, and it just spread through the dining room. We'll not repeat that performance."

"I'll say you won't repeat it!" bellowed Mr. Fairchild. "The Magruders won't even be *around* to repeat it."

Mrs. Magruder began to weep.

"Why, it's getting to the point where people come to the Bessledorf just to see what's going to happen next," Mr. Fairchild went on. "Story like this hits the papers, and you'll have people lining up outside just to . . . uh. . . ." He paused. "How many people did you have in the dining room last night?"

"A hundred and eight, sir—filled to capacity—with a line in the lobby."

"You don't say?" said Mr. Fairchild, and his voice softened noticeably. "Well, don't just sit there with your teeth in your mouth. What have you got lined up for next weekend?"

The Magruders all looked at each other. Mother stopped crying.

"Why . . . uh . . . uh. . . . We've got a new combo ready to go, sir," stammered Joseph.

Bernie stared at him.

"A new combo, huh? C as in clarinet, O as in oboe, M as in marimba, B as in bass, and O as in out-in-the-street, which is where you'll be if it isn't a success?"

"Uh . . . yes, sir. We don't have those same instruments exactly, but it *is* a good group."

Bernie raised his eyebrows.

"What kind of music does it play?" asked Fairchild.

"Dixieland," Joseph answered, as his father's mouth opened in astonishment.

"Very good. Very good indeed," said Mr. Fairchild. "What's the name of the group?"

"The name?" Joseph looked around desperately. Lewis and Clark wandered into the kitchen and rubbed up against his legs. "Oh, the name of the group is . . . uh . . . the Cat's Pajamas," Joseph announced.

12

The Cat's Pajamas

It wasn't enough that a body was found in the bathtub, Bernie thought. Wasn't enough that another was found on the floor. The night before, someone had shouted out an insult in the dining room, and then there was whipped cream all over the place. Too many things were happening one after another to be coincidence. It seemed to Bernie, and Officer Feeney, too, that someone was trying to put the Bessledorf out of business. Maybe a lot of someones. And now Joseph was getting involved just to save his father's job.

"Joseph, what have you done?" Mrs. Magruder asked. "What did you promise Mr. Fairchild?"

"I had to say something, Mother," Joseph told her.

"But where did you find a combo called the Cat's Pajamas?"

Joseph shrugged. "I didn't exactly find one, but here are a couple of guys at the veterinary college who play instruments."

Delores rolled her eyes. "Like a bird surgeon blowing a dog whistle?"

"Not quite," said Joseph. "But we do have a horse doctor who's pretty good on the trumpet and a feline dermatologist who plays the saxophone."

"That's a combo?" said Mr. Magruder.

"The driver of the van plays the drums," Joseph added, "and I thought maybe I'd play my trombone."

"But have you ever practiced together?" asked his mother.

"No, but we might as well give it a try."

Bernie couldn't stand to listen. It was time for action. He called up Georgene and Weasel, and they all met at the top of Bessledorf Hill with their skateboards.

"Someone," Bernie told them, "is trying to put the Bessledorf out of business. I'm sure of it. And we've only got a week to find him. Next Friday night Joseph and some friends are going to perform in the hotel dining room, and it's sure to be a disaster."

"What do you want us to do?" asked Georgene.

"I'll be looking for Phillip Gusset, the first guest who disappeared; Weasel, you look for the man with the big nose who started throwing the whipped cream last night; and Georgene, you keep your eye out for that orange-haired woman with the green glasses. We ought to spot at least one of them."

They started out at the top of the hill and rolled downward, checking out everyone on the sidewalk. Weasel made it as far as the bus depot, Georgene made it as far as the funeral home, and Bernie went all the way to the deli. If he could just add another five blocks, he might write to *The Guinness Book of World Records* to see if anyone had ever beat his distance. But right now there were more important things to do.

They didn't have much luck. In the bus depot alone, there were five men with mustaches, and four others had big noses and thick glasses.

"I don't see anyone who looks like the man I saw last night," said Weasel.

And nobody saw any woman with orange hair.

They walked through the library, skateboards under their arms, circled the park, meandered through City Hall. They checked out the bookstore, the drugstore, the supermart, and the bowling alley.

"Even if we found one of them, what would we do?" asked Weasel finally. "We can't have them arrested because we don't have any evidence against them; we can't follow them around all the time because most of the time we're in school; we can't . . ."

"All we need to do is find out where they're

staying, and then ask Feeney to keep an eye on them for us," said Bernie.

After several hours of searching, however, they gave up; and Bernie went to bed that evening feeling very discouraged.

Lester was worried, too.

"Bernie," he said in the dark from the top bunk. "If Dad loses his job, where do you suppose we'll go?"

"The poorhouse," said Bernie darkly.

"What's it like in the poorhouse?"

"Awful," said Bernie. "You have to wear old clothes with patches, and for dinner you get whatever the rich people have left over. You'd hate it, Les."

Lester began to sniffle.

"Don't worry," Bernie reassured him. "Rich people always have a lot left over. Besides, Dad will think of something." But he didn't feel hopeful at all.

When Bernie got home from school on Monday, he opened the door of the hotel and was met with a dreadful noise. It seemed to be coming from the basement.

"What *is* it?" he asked his mother, who was on duty at the front desk. Mrs. Magruder was writing the second chapter of her romance novel, and she had papers spread out all over the desk.

"The Cat's Pajamas—their first rehearsal," she told him, and went on writing.

"But it's terrible!" protested Bernie.

"I know," she said. "Joseph says they'll be much improved by Friday, but I doubt it." She sat tapping her pencil against the desk, a faraway look in her eyes. "I think," she said aloud, "I will make the hero in my story have a peg leg. I've always wanted to meet a man with a peg leg."

There were times that Bernie did not understand his mother. If she wanted to meet a man with a yacht, or a man who looked like a movie star, or a man who played the guitar beneath her window, Bernie might understand that. But he did not know why anyone would be especially thrilled to meet a man with only one leg.

"Why?" he asked her.

"Oh, I don't know, dear. It's just that you don't see a man with a peg leg every day."

"You don't see a man with only one ear, either," Bernie told her, "but you never write about that." His mother didn't even hear him.

Just then a man came in the front door with a suitcase. He had curly blond hair and a huge blond beard that completely covered his chin and neck. Over his left eye, he wore a black eye patch. Bernie couldn't help staring. Mother stared, too.

"I'd like a first floor room," the man said to Mother. He looked around dubiously. "A *quiet* room, if there is one."

"All of our rooms are quiet, sir," Mother shouted over the noise of the rehearsal. "I assure you that the noise coming from the basement will stop shortly. However, I will put you as far away from it as possible."

Henry Brown, the man wrote in the guest book, and took the key that Mrs. Magruder handed to him.

"Down that hall," she directed. "Bernie, will you take Mr. Brown's suitcase, please?" Her eyes followed him with that faraway look that bothered Bernie.

The man started off down the hall, and as Bernie bent to pick up his suitcase, he heard his mother whisper, as if to herself, "Heliotrope."

13

Heliotrope

Bernie began putting things together in his head. There were only two other guests who had reminded his mother of heliotrope—Phillip Gusset and Ethel King—and both of them had disappeared. If anyone was going to disappear next, it should be this man called Henry Brown with the blond beard and black eye patch. Bernie almost wished that he would.

He watched as the man walked around room 114. Mr. Brown went to the window and looked out, then turned suddenly and handed Bernie a quarter. His dark eyes looked down at him, and Bernie had the feeling that even the eye beneath the patch was watching him intently.

He went back down the hall to the lobby. Hildegarde was just finishing up, putting her bucket in the broom closet.

"Hildegarde," Bernie whispered, leaning against the doorframe. "I think I know where the next body's going to turn up."

The red-haired woman whirled around, her lips shaped in a huge *O*.

"Lord o'mercy," she cried, one hand to her throat.

"Listen, I need your help," Bernie went on. "I think that someone is trying to close down the Bessledorf, and I don't think that the bodies we've found were dead at all—not one bit."

Hildegarde's eyes grew wider.

"I have a hunch," said Bernie, "that the man who just checked into room 114 is going to play dead next."

Hildegarde sat down on top of her bucket, her breath coming in short gasps.

"The next time you open a door to a room, *any* room, and see a body lying there, don't scream,"

Bernie told her. "Don't even leave. Don't take your eyes off it for a moment."

"Oh, no!" said Hildegarde. "Not this girl! I'm not passin' the time of day with no spirits."

"You don't have to stay very long," Bernie said, looking around the broom closet. His eyes fell on Hildegarde's coat and hat hanging on a hook on the door. He reached up and pulled out the big hatpin that Hildegarde used on windy days.

"Here's what you do," said Bernie. "Wear this pin on your apron every day, and if you walk into a room with a body in it, you just ever so gently go up and stick the pin in one toe."

Hildegarde almost slid off the bucket.

"No *way*, Bernie Magruder!" she gasped. "I'm not about to go stickin' pins in corpses."

"Please, Hildegarde! You just might save the hotel. You certainly will save my dad's job if we can find the person who's behind all this."

Hildegarde shook her head violently.

"You'd get your name in all the newspapers. You'd even be on television."

Hildegarde stopped shaking her head. "TV, you say? The Tonight Show, maybe?"

"Sure," said Bernie, even though he wasn't.

Hildegarde smiled just a little. "Well, now, I always did sort of fancy myself on TV; but I swear, Bernie, I'd be shaking so if I met a corpse I wouldn't be able to stick a pin in the side of a barn door."

"I tell you what," said Bernie. "When do you start cleaning rooms each morning?"

"About eight-thirty," said Hildegarde.

"All right. Every morning you start with room 114 just before I leave for school. Then I'll be here in case you need me."

"All right," Hildegarde promised.

When Bernie came home from school on Tuesday, the Cat's Pajamas were practicing again. They sounded only a little better. Bernie picked up Lewis and Clark, one in each arm, and sat at the top of the basement stairs to watch the rehearsal. But the cats laid their ears back, fluffed their tails, and squirmed out of Bernie's arms, escaping to the lobby.

Wednesday morning, Bernie waited at the end of the hall while Hildegarde tapped on the door of room 114, then went inside. A minute later she came to the doorway and waved Bernie on, and he knew that there was no body on the floor that day.

"How are the Cat's Pajamas coming along?" Georgene asked him at lunchtime.

"Don't ask," said Bernie, moodily munching his tuna sandwich.

"I think you ought to have Officer Feeney right there in the dining room when they start to play," Weasel suggested. "Just in case somebody starts tossing chairs or something."

Bernie didn't feel a bit better.

When he got home that afternoon, the Cat's Pajamas were at it again, and Mr. Magruder sat at the front desk wearing earplugs. He didn't even hear Bernie come in, so Bernie went on back to the apartment.

At the door of the kitchen, he stopped, for his mother was standing by the table reading a letter. Her lips were slightly parted, her cheeks were pink, and the hand that rested on her chest rose up and down with each breath she took. She stopped reading after a moment, held the letter against her, eyes staring off into the distance, then read it all over again. This time her cheeks grew pinker still.

Bernie tried to walk in without startling her.

"Hi, Mom," he said casually, and reached for the peanut butter and crackers.

Hurriedly, Mrs. Magruder tucked the letter up one sleeve of her blouse.

"Hello, Bernie," she said and quickly turned her back on him. "How was school?"

"Okay. Anything exciting happen here?"

"Why, no. Why do you ask?" She turned and looked at him strangely.

Bernie shrugged. "Just wondered." He opened the jar and began spreading peanut butter thickly on his crackers.

Later that afternoon, however, as he was crossing the lobby, he found a small piece of paper, folded, that looked like the letter his mother had been reading.

He picked it up. What should he do now? He wasn't *sure* it was his mother's letter. But how would he know unless he looked? Slowly he unfolded it. He would read only enough to see whose name was at the top.

"My dearest Alma," the letter began, and before Bernie could fold it back up, his eyes had scanned the whole thing:

I don't know if you have thought of me at all over the years, but I have never watched a sunset or a sunrise without thinking of you. Let me take you away from all your troubles at the Bessledorf and treat you like the princess you deserve to be.

I cannot live without you. If your answer is no, my fate is sealed, and I shall no doubt do something desperate. But if you can find it in your heart to go off with me, take the rose enclosed in this letter, place it in a vase, and set it in the second floor window just above the hotel canopy.

A thousand kisses await you from your old flame.

Jackson Prather

14

One Thousand Kisses

Bernie sat silent and still on a chair in the corner of the lobby. His stomach felt like a load of wet clothes at the bottom of the dryer. Every time he looked at his father there at the front desk and thought about what he knew that his father didn't, his stomach whirled around again and settled once more, damp and heavy.

There was a lot he didn't know about his mother, he decided. He didn't know anything about Jackson Prather, either, except that he didn't like him at all.

Why did the man wait all these years until things were at their worst? Whoever he was,

Jackson Prather must have read the news stories about bodies disappearing at the Bessledorf. And somehow he had kept track of Bernie's mother all this time and knew that she was here.

Mr. Lamkin wandered into the lobby and turned on the TV. The program was *No Tomorrow,* the old man's favorite soap opera, and there on the screen was a blonde woman named Constance Cornwall who was telling her husband that she was running off to Tuscaloosa with a carnival man. Mr. Lamkin pulled out his handkerchief and wiped his eyes. Bernie felt like crying, too.

In the apartment kitchen that evening, Mrs. Magruder quietly served dinner, her lips pursed as though she were deep in thought, her cheeks still pink. On the shelf above the sink, a red rose sat in a small vase. No one seemed to have noticed the rose except Bernie.

"Oh, what a day!" Delores was saying, pouring catsup on her french fries and passing the bottle on around the table. "I don't think we finished a single parachute at the factory. All anyone wanted to talk about was what's been happening here at the hotel. I got so nervous and flustered that I dropped the grommets all over the floor and sewed the harness straps on backward. It's a wonder I didn't get fired."

"Don't even mention that word," said her father. "*Someone* around here has to have a job." He sighed and reached across the table, putting one hand on top of Mrs. Magruder's. "I wonder what you ever saw in me, Alma. Here we are, never knowing from one week to the next whether we'll be out on the street or not."

Bernie watched his mother. They *all* watched Mother. Surely she would say something reassuring, something to make her husband feel better. But Mrs. Magruder just put her other hand on top of Father's, like a three-decker sandwich, and pretty soon the catsup came down her side of the table, and everyone began eating again.

"Don't worry, Dad," Joseph told him. "The Cat's Pajamas are almost ready for Friday night. We'll bring business back to the Bessledorf again."

"It won't do any good if the guest list keeps dropping," Theodore said. "Even if the dining room was filled every Friday and Saturday night, we'd lose money if the rooms went vacant."

"We could start a haunted house!" Lester said, shaking the catsup bottle so hard that his plate looked like a surgical operation. "We could sell tickets and take people on tours and show them the rooms where the bodies were found."

"Just finish your dinner, Lester," said Mr. Magruder, and then there was no sound in the kitchen but the clink of knives and forks against the plates.

At the front desk later, Bernie sat down beside his father.

"Need any help, Dad?" he asked. "I could add up the week's receipts."

"There weren't that many," said Mr. Magruder. "I could almost add them on my fingers."

"Want me to straighten up your paper clip drawer or something?"

"I've already done that," his father told him. "I

have straightened the drawers, sharpened my pencils, balanced the books, laundered the towels, and watered the begonias. There isn't that much to do around here with no new guests at the Bessledorf."

"Then I'll just sit here and keep you company," said Bernie. They watched Mixed Blessing scratch himself on the mat by the door and Salt Water pace back and forth on his perch. The only real action in the lobby that evening was from Lewis and Clark, who pounced on each other from behind the curtains.

"Dad," Bernie said after a bit, "what do you think about when you watch the sun rise?"

"Whether I'll be able to pay all my bills," said his father.

"Well, what do you think about when you see the sun *set*?"

"That it's another day down the tube," said Mr. Magruder. "Why?"

No wonder Mom had that faraway look in her eye, Bernie thought.

"Did you ever call anyone princess or send her a rose or tell her that a thousand kisses were waiting for her?" he asked.

Mr. Magruder turned around and looked at Bernie. "You wouldn't happen to be in love, would you?"

"I'm asking *you*," said Bernie.

"Oh, I suppose I did once when I was courting your mother—give her flowers or something. A thousand kisses is a whole lot of kisses, though, I can tell you that."

15

The Window on the Second Floor

Bernie stayed up that night as long as he could, keeping an eye on his mother. When he went to bed at last, he was afraid to go to sleep. He imagined waking up in the morning to find his mother gone, taking her romance novels with her, and Delores making breakfast for the family. The year before, Delores had almost married a man from Hoboken, New Jersey, but the wedding never came off. Maybe, Bernie was thinking, he could get Delores and Jackson Prather together somehow. If Delores would run off with Mother's old flame, then everyone would be happy. Except, perhaps, Mother. The worry started inside him again.

He heard a sound like the snapping of a suitcase. Slowly he got out of bed and opened the bedroom door just a crack. It was only Mixed Blessing, shaking his flea collar.

Bernie lay back down and stared at the ceiling. How could he tell Mother he wanted her to stay without admitting that he had read her letter? He heard another sound, like someone tiptoeing to the hall closet to get her coat. But when he got up to check, he found only Lewis and Clark playing around the galoshes.

He could not help worrying about what would happen the next day when he and his brothers and sister were out of the house. Maybe he could ask Hildegarde to keep an eye on Mother. Or tell Wilbur Wilkins, the handyman, that if he saw a suspicious man hanging around, he should tell Father at once. Bernie got up again and looked out the window to see if anyone was waiting about now, then lay back down.

"What's wrong?" Lester asked from the top bunk.

For once Bernie actually felt sorry for his younger brother. He didn't know how to tell him that maybe when he came home from school the following day their mother would be gone.

"Lester," Bernie said. "No matter what happens, you'll still have a father."

"What?" said Lester.

"Nothing," Bernie told him and rolled over, but it was a long time before he slept.

When he got up the next morning, he checked the kitchen. Both his mother and the rose were still there.

"That flower looks sort of wilted," Bernie said as he poured his shredded wheat. "Maybe you ought to throw it out."

"Oh, I think I'll keep it awhile longer," said Mrs. Magruder, and she paused, with the faraway look in her eye.

"Maybe you could give it to Delores," Bernie said brightly. "*She* loves flowers."

"No," said Mother, "I think I'll keep this one myself."

The shredded wheat in Bernie's mouth tasted like wood shavings, and he swallowed without chewing.

At school, he could not tell Georgene and Weasel what had happened. He could tell them about disappearing bodies, but he could not tell them about Jackson Prather and his thousand kisses. As soon as he got home, he went again to the kitchen. His mother and the rose were still there.

The Cat's Pajamas were having their last rehearsal before the performance on Friday. Bernie wasn't sure if they sounded any better or not. Mixed Blessing lifted his head every so often from the mat by the front door and howled.

Bernie went up to the second floor, to the little hall window just above the hotel canopy, and sat down on the window seat. He knew that as long as he was there, at least, his mother would not try to put the rose in the window. And if the rose was not in the window, Jackson Prather, whoever he was, would not have the signal he wanted.

Bernie sat on the window seat until dinnertime, then went back to sit some more. Sometimes people on the street below glanced up and saw him there, but none of them looked the way Bernie imagined Jackson Prather to look.

About nine, just as he was getting ready to quit for the evening, Bernie heard the stairwell door open softly at the end of the corridor. Then it closed slowly again. Someone had started to enter the hall, seen Bernie, and gone back out.

Bernie ran as fast as he could to the end of the hall and opened the door, but the stairs were empty. When he walked in the apartment a few minutes later, his mother was standing by the sink in the kitchen, the rose in her hand.

16

Dead

As he was dressing for school on Friday, Bernie thought of going down to the kitchen, taking the rose, and tossing it in the trash. He wanted it out of the house. Somehow he knew that whatever was going to happen next would happen that very day.

Phillip Gusset was still about, he was sure. And probably Ethel King. When the Cat's Pajamas performed in the dining room that night, there was sure to be some horrible disturbance. It would make the Saturday morning newspaper in Indianapolis, Mr. Fairchild would fire Bernie's father, and Mother would decide she had had enough and ride off into the sunset with her old flame, Jackson Prather. Bernie would be a one-half orphan. He wiped away a tear as he combed his hair. He had to get rid of the rose.

When he got to the breakfast table, however, the rose was not on the shelf. Whirling around, Bernie rushed wildly back through the lobby, almost colliding with Hildegarde, and went racing up the stairs to the second floor. But there was no vase in the window above the canopy, no rose. Bernie went back down.

Mrs. Magruder was putting French toast on the table and when she turned, Bernie saw that the rose was pinned to the front of her lavender dress—right over her heart.

Slowly he sat down at his place and watched her.

"Pretty flower, Alma," said Mr. Magruder to his wife as she poured his coffee.

"Thank you," said Mother.

"Where did you get it?" asked Delores through a yawn.

"Oh, it just turned up," said Mrs. Magruder,

and she changed the conversation to other things.

Bernie sat in the lobby waiting until it was time to go to school. The rose on his mother's dress seemed even more ominous than if it had been in the second floor window. Maybe Jackson Prather had come in the night to see her. Maybe this was a new sign, a sign that her bags were packed and she was ready to go. As soon as Delores was off to the parachute factory and Joseph was off to the veterinary college and Bernie and Lester had gone to school, Bernie's mother might just slip out the back door with her bags and boxes, hop in the car of her old flame, and roar off forever.

As it happened, however, Mrs. Magruder did not ride off into the sunset. She didn't even leave the hotel. Neither did Bernie.

Far down at the end of the west corridor, Hildegarde had begun her morning cleaning. As she had promised Bernie, she started with Henry Brown's room.

From his chair beside Salt Water's perch, Bernie saw Hildegarde tap on the door of room 114, wait, then call out, "It's all right, sir. I'll come back later."

She motioned to Bernie, and he met her halfway down the corridor.

"Always before, he's out having his breakfast," she whispered. "Sure as I'm standin' here, I come back to clean his room later, and there'll be a body in it."

"Do you have your hat pin with you?" Bernie asked.

Hildegarde patted her apron.

"Then just do what I told you. If you walk in Henry Brown's room and he looks like he's dead, don't you leave him for a minute. You just stick your hatpin a little way in one of his feet. If he has his shoes on, you stick it in one thumb. That'll bring him back to life in a hurry."

"Oh, Bernie, I can't."

"You *have* to, Hildegarde. I can't stay any longer. I've got to get to school."

Hildegarde gave a resigned sigh, nodded bravely, and went back to tap on the next door. Bernie tucked his books under his arm and set off. Behind him, he heard the jangle of Hildegarde's keys as she opened the door next to Henry Brown's room. And then, just as Bernie was about to turn the corner, he heard the patter of footsteps behind him and saw Hildegarde, her face white, motioning him back.

He ran.

"It's there, in *that* room! A b . . . body!" she stammered.

"Shh. Did you stick a pin in it?"

"Lordy, no!"

Bernie walked through the door of the room.

There was a body, all right. It was a small man, about seventy, wrapped in a sheet; and he lay stiffly, gray as an old work shirt, on the bed, his bare feet pointing outward.

"Lord have mercy," Hildegarde breathed, crossing herself.

"He sure looks dead," said Bernie, "but they all looked dead."

He walked over to the bed, heart pounding.

"Sir? It's eight-thirty. Are you ready for coffee?" Bernie asked.

The little man on the bed did not stir.

"Are you all right, Mister?" Bernie asked, bending down and talking right in the man's ear.

The body did not move.

Bernie's heart began to pump painfully inside him, and his breath caught in his throat.

"Give me the hatpin," he said to Hildegarde.

Covering her eyes with one hand, Hildegarde passed him the pin.

With shaking fingers, Bernie took the pin and pricked the big toe of the man there on the bed. The body did not move. The foot did not twitch. The big toe did not even bleed.

Hildegarde, who had been peeping through her finger, began backing toward the door.

Maybe it's a wax figure, a department store dummy, Bernie thought. He moved toward the man's head and, with one thumb, lifted the eyelid. A green watery eye stared dully back at him. The skin felt cold.

The man was dead.

17

The Missing Body

Bernie was still afraid that if he went to get his father, the body on the bed would disappear.

"Go get my dad," he told Hildegarde. "Walk slowly, speak quietly, and don't let *anyone* know what's happened."

No sooner had Hildegarde left the room, however, her hair flying, her face white, than somebody else came in. It was Henry Brown from next door.

"What's all the commotion?" he asked, looking puzzled. Then, seeing the body on the bed, "Hey! What's going on?"

"That's what we're about to find out," said Bernie. "The police should be here shortly."

"Heart attack?" asked Mr. Brown, walking over to the bed and looking down at the old man.

"I don't know," said Bernie, suspicious of this snoopy stranger. "Maybe it's murder."

"Murder! You don't say! This hotel has quite a reputation, doesn't it?"

"It's not the hotel, it's the people who stay in it," Bernie said hotly and would have said more, but at that moment Theodore Magruder strode quickly into the room.

"So we've finally caught one," he said, staring at the body on the bed and then at Mr. Brown. "May I ask what you are doing here, sir?"

The blond man with the black eye patch stroked his beard. "I heard a commotion in this room and decided to check it out," he said.

"What kind of commotion?" Mr. Magruder asked. "Shouting? Gunshots? Scuffling?"

"There wasn't any commotion at all," said Bernie angrily. "Hildegarde and I were talking to each other, that's all."

"Well, their voices certainly sounded excited," said Mr. Brown. "But if you don't care for my opinion, I'll leave."

"Everybody stay right where you are," said Officer Feeney, coming through the doorway. Following close behind him was Mr. Coldwater, the mortician.

"That's him!" Mr. Coldwater exclaimed excitedly. "That's my body! He disappeared from the funeral parlor, and we didn't discover it until this morning. The funeral's set for one o'clock, and we've got to have the man dressed, shaved, and manicured before the relatives arrive. Why, he was about to be late for his own funeral!"

"How do you explain this, Magruder?" asked Feeney, looking at Father and taking out his notebook and pen.

"How can I explain anything that's been happening around here?" said Mr. Magruder helplessly. "This room isn't even supposed to be occupied. There is no guest registered for room 116. Someone broke into your funeral home in the

116

night, Mr. Coldwater, borrowed this body, and brought it here; how or why I can't tell you. But the shock to my poor cleaning woman has almost put her under."

"Oh, don't say 'under,' sir," Hildegarde wept from the doorway.

Officer Feeney turned to Henry Brown. "Did you hear anything in the night? A window being opened? Footsteps outside? Voices, even?"

"Not a thing," said Henry Brown. "I was awake until early this morning reading a book, and I can assure you that if there were any unusual goings-on outside, I would have known. Obviously," he added, looking straight at Bernie's father, "this is an inside job. But when a hotel goes in for body snatching, there's something sick and sinful about the place, if you ask me."

"Can I quote you on that, sir?" asked a voice from the doorway, where a group of newspaper reporters were waiting; and as the body was wheeled outside on a stretcher, flashbulbs popped, reporters scribbled, and Felicity Jones, Mr. Lamkin, and Mrs. Buzzwell watched the procession from the doorways of their rooms.

Felicity, of course, had composed another poem while all the fuss was going on, and read it aloud as the procession passed:

> "He didn't belong in this hallway,
> He didn't belong on that bed;
> And though you might say he's intruding,
> You'll have to admit he's quite dead."

Bernie decided it was better than her other poems. At least she'd left out the angels and zephyrs. But when a reporter asked permission to reprint it, he felt angry all over again. No matter what happened at the Bessledorf, it was sure to be in the newspapers the following day.

As the corpse was wheeled out the front door, guests watched from the hotel dining room, the lobby, and the elevator. By the time Feeney wrote up his report, a line of people had gathered at the registration desk to check out.

Bernie stayed home from school all day to help his

father, and by lunchtime, there were no guests left in the Bessledorf but Henry Brown and the regulars.

"Don't tell me you're not checking out, too?" Mr. Magruder said as Henry Brown passed him in the lobby.

"I have the feeling, sir, that I am under suspicion in this sordid affair, and Henry Brown has never been one to run away until his innocence has been proved," the man said. "Distressing as it is to me, I will stay until I have my good name back once more." And he swept grandly on into the dining room.

Mrs. Magruder began to weep, and Mr. Magruder put his arms round her. "Oh, Alma, so it's come to this, then. My dream of managing our own hotel is over, and soon there will be not a soul left, not even the regulars."

"Whatever will become of us?" Mother sobbed, as Bernie watched helplessly from a chair in the corner. "Where will we go? We have the children to think of. We can't just see them turned out onto the street."

"We will carry on at least through tonight," said Mr. Magruder. "We promised the public the Cat's Pajamas, and the Cat's Pajamas they shall have. Either it will be the Bessledorf's finest hour, and Joseph and his friends will somehow redeem us all, or it will be the last disaster, and the Bessledorf will close its doors. We could always go live with my sister in Ohio."

"Not that bubblehead!" exclaimed Mother. "Never, Theodore!" She pushed away from him and marched back into the apartment.

It was the first time Bernie had ever heard his mother call someone a bubblehead. He scrunched down farther into the big chair and closed his eyes. She would be leaving for sure.

"Nothing worse could possibly happen," he said to Lewis and Clark as they climbed onto his lap.

But something worse *did* happen. A cab pulled up, a man got out, and a moment later the door of the hotel flew open and in walked Robert L. Fairchild himself.

18

Robert L. Fairchild Himself

He wore a gray flannel suit and a red-and-blue tie and a watch chain that swung from his vest pocket with every step.

"It's gone far enough," said Mr. Fairchild, tapping his cane on the floor and striding up to the front desk. "When I read it in the newspapers, that's one thing, but when the chief of police of Middleburg calls me long-distance to say there's a bona fide corpse in my hotel, that's the last straw. Over, finished, and done with."

"What do you mean?" asked Mr. Magruder, his face ashen, as his wife came back out of the apartment and watched timidly from the doorway.

"I mean that I have hired someone else for your position as manager of this hotel. I want you Magruders out of here by three o'clock Sunday afternoon, and not a minute later."

It seemed to Bernie, sitting in one corner of the lobby with his two cats, that the chair or his stomach or both were sinking right through the floor, and the hotel was collapsing around him. He imagined them all getting on a bus come Sunday afternoon, with Lewis and Clark, Mixed Blessing, Salt Water, and a dozen bags and boxes, and going off to Ohio to live with Father's sister. He didn't even remember his Aunt Sally, who according to Mother, was a bubblehead. The Magruders had moved so often, due to Mr. Magruder's many jobs, that Bernie mixed up aunts with teachers, uncles with moving men, and grandparents with all the little old men and women he had seen waiting in train stations. They had moved so much that Bernie scarcely memorized one address and telephone number before he had to remember another.

"Should we go ahead with the entertainment planned for this evening?" Mr. Magruder asked. There was no fight left in him, no sparkle in his eyes, no starch in his shoulders.

"Yes, yes, of course you must go ahead with the program," said Mr. Fairchild, and his voice softened slightly. "I'm really sorry to have to do this, Theodore. I've no doubt you're good people—try to do your best and all that. But sometimes the best isn't enough. Things keep happening; I don't know why, and you don't know why, and the police don't know why, so it seems to me it would be better all around to end the jinx and start out with a new manager. I've got a man coming in Sunday, and of course he'll need your apartment."

Mr. Magruder nodded, and Mrs. Magruder dabbed at her eyes with a handkerchief.

"Now," said Mr. Fairchild, "I would like you to show me, room by room, floor by floor, just where all the mysterious bodies have been found."

Mrs. Magruder went back to the apartment to begin packing up, but Bernie followed after his father as they went first to the room of Phillip A. Gusset.

Mr. Magruder explained how Hildegarde had found the body in the bathtub and how, when the Magruders got back to the room, the man had disappeared.

"Extraordinary," said Mr. Fairchild.

"Gusset and his clothes along with him," said Mr. Magruder.

"Uh . . . not quite, Dad," Bernie put in. "There's something you should know."

Both Mr. Magruder and Mr. Fairchild turned and stared at him.

"When I was looking around his room just after Hildegarde found the body, I saw a pair of old brown slippers under the bed," Bernie told them. "But in all the excitement of the body being missing, I forgot to tell you. When I thought of it later and went back to get them for fingerprints or something, they were gone."

"What?" said Mr. Magruder. "Why didn't you tell me then?"

Bernie felt miserable. "Because you seemed so upset already."

Mr. Fairchild's eyes darted about and he seemed almost to hop with excitement. "Now who would want a pair of old slippers? If *you* didn't take them and the cleaning woman and the police didn't take them, then the only person who would want them would be Gusset himself."

"Exactly," said Mr. Magruder, but his voice was flat. Bernie could tell he was thinking about moving his family to Ohio. He just didn't care anymore about the mystery.

"By Jove, I *like* being a detective!" said Mr. Fairchild, and his eyes began to dance. "I should have come down here sooner. It is reasonable to assume, therefore, that Phillip A. Gusset is alive and well and probably living in Middleburg."

"Quite," said Mr. Magruder.

"Onward!" cried Mr. Fairchild, raising his cane and pointing toward the door. "To the next room."

They went to Ethel King's room next.

"Was anything left behind in this room?" Mr. Fairchild asked, looking at Bernie.

"I don't think so, sir. But she left without paying her bill, and her window was open. She had even asked for a room with a fire escape."

"Premeditated thievery," said Fairchild. "The woman knew when she checked in that she would leave without paying. Scoundrels, both of them. Now, about the third . . ."

"I can't tell you much about the gentleman from the funeral parlor," said Mr. Magruder. "All we know is that somehow he got from the funeral home into this hotel. His liver, I think."

"His liver was in this hotel?"

"No, his liver was what did him in, I believe. And here he was, stretched out on one of our beds while they searched for him next door."

"Somebody must have carried him in," said Mr. Fairchild. "He certainly didn't walk in here by himself."

"Our deduction exactly," said Mr. Magruder.

"Why, if I knew the ins and outs of the detective

business, I just might have come down to Middleburg at the first disappearance and taken over the case myself," said Mr. Fairchild. "Now I know you folks have a lot to do, what with getting ready for the program tonight and packing to leave and all, so you just go on about your business. It's a shame things didn't turn out better. A pity."

And tapping his cane on the floor once more, he went outside for his afternoon walk.

Bernie followed his parents around the apartment. His mother's face was grim. The rose that had been pinned to her blouse that morning was faded and shriveled, but it was still there.

"I absolutely cannot bear the thought of moving again, Theodore," Mother said. "If I had only known, twenty-three years ago when I married you, what I was in for . . ."

"I know, I know," said Bernie's father, but there was anger in his voice as well. "Say it, Alma. Come right out and say it. If you had married that pig Jackson Prather when he asked you, your life would be different today."

Bernie stopped in his tracks, listening.

"He was not a pig, Theodore. He was a gentleman. He took me rowing and let me sit on his jacket."

"He never changed his shirts and his armpits stank," said Mr. Magruder.

"He brought me chocolates in a gold-and-silver box," said Mother.

"He ate limburger cheese with his mouth open," said Mr. Magruder.

Mother turned and faced him. Her neck grew pink and her cheeks even pinker, and suddenly she started to cry. She whirled about and rushed into the bedroom, shutting the door behind her. Bernie felt sick.

19

Sacked

If his mother was ever going to leave the family and run off with Jackson Prather, it was now, this very minute, Bernie thought.

He spent the rest of the afternoon sitting on the window seat on the second floor, just above the hotel canopy, watching the street below. Every time a man stopped and looked up, even stopped at all, Bernie was ready to rush out and flatten him to the sidewalk. The Magruders might be on their way to the poorhouse, but Bernie wouldn't give up his mother without a fight.

Around two o'clock, Mrs. Magruder came upstairs to see about linens and noticed Bernie at the window in the hallway. She still had Jackson Prather's rose pinned to her dress.

"What are you doing here Bernie?" she asked.

"Nothing," he said morosely.

She paused and put one hand on his shoulder. "You should have gone to school today. In all the commotion, I just didn't think."

"It's okay," Bernie told her. "I don't think I missed anything important." He wanted to ask her about Jackson Prather and his thousand kisses, but he couldn't find the right words so he asked, instead, "Mom, do you think you'll be happy in Ohio?"

Mrs. Magruder took her hand off Bernie's shoulder. "I have no intention of going to Ohio," she said. "Something will turn up yet." And with that she walked quickly on up the hall.

Bernie wandered down to the lobby about three where old Mr. Lamkin was watching television. There was a mid-afternoon news break in which they announced that a corpse had been found that morning in the Bessledorf Hotel. Full details at six, the announcer added. Bernie turned away.

Lester came home from school and announced that *everybody* was talking about the new body in the Bessledorf Hotel. Bernie followed him out to the kitchen, wondering how to tell his young brother that their father had been fired.

"Les," he said finally, as Lester prepared to make himself a grape milkshake, "I'm afraid the worst has happened: Dad's been sacked."

Lester turned and stared at him. For a long time he stood there without saying a word. Then he dished up a half cup of grape jelly and dropped it in the blender.

"When are we leaving?" Lester asked in a tiny little voice, pouring in a can of grape juice.

"Sunday."

"Where are we going?" Lester wanted to know, adding a scoop of chocolate ice cream.

"Ohio, I guess."

Lester added a package of grape Kool-Aid. "Is Mom coming with us?" he asked. So Lester had noticed, too!

"I don't know," said Bernie.

Lester flipped the switch on the blender and the stuff inside turned gray. That was how he felt himself, Bernie thought: gray and cold and awful. He tried not to watch while Lester drank his mixture. Afterward, as Lester wiped his mouth on his T-shirt, Bernie saw that he was wiping his eyes as well.

"I wouldn't mind going to the poorhouse, Bernie, if Mom was there," Lester sniffled, "but I don't want to go any place, not even Ohio, if she's not along."

Bernie put one arm around him comfortingly. "We'll see," he said.

Georgene Riley and Weasel came by later with their skateboards.

"We wondered if you were sick," Weasel told him. "Then somebody heard about the corpse, and we figured that's why you were absent. What did it look like, Bernie?"

"Dead," said Bernie. "Very dead."

"Weren't you scared?" Georgene questioned.

Bernie really didn't want to talk about it. "I'm more scared of what's going to happen to Dad," he told them. "Mr. Fairchild flew down here from Indianapolis, and he says a new manager is taking over on Sunday. Dad's been sacked."

Georgene dropped her skateboard and stared at him. "Bernie, what will you do?"

Bernie shrugged and swallowed. "Dad's talking about moving to Ohio," he told them.

"Oh, Bernie, don't go!" Georgene begged. "You could come and live with us. You could sleep on our sofa."

"You could live at our house, too," Weasel said. "I'll ask Mom if you could room with me."

Bernie shook his head. "I've got to stay with the family," he told them.

"Well, we've got to do something," said Weasel, and started thinking of all the things they could *not* do. "We can't get rid of Mr. Fairchild because he owns the place; we can't ask him not to fire your father because he already has; we can't . . ."

"If we could just find out who brought that

corpse into the hotel last night, we might have the answer to what's been happening here," Bernie interrupted. "And if we had the answer, it just might be that Fairchild would let us stay."

"But how can we help?" Georgene wanted to know.

"Listen," said Bernie. "I have the feeling that Henry Brown is about to disappear next. I want you to watch his room. One of you can sit in the lobby and keep an eye on his door, and the other can sit out in the alley and watch his window. If you see anything at all unusual, let me know."

"Where will you be?" asked Georgene.

Bernie stared down at his feet. "I'll be sitting in the second floor window just above the canopy. I have the feeling that something big is going to happen out on the sidewalk. I'll explain later."

So Georgene found a chair in the lobby where she could see down the west hall to Mr. Brown's room, and Weasel went out and sat on the wall by the alley. Bernie took up his watch again at the window on the second floor.

From time to time Mr. Lamkin and Mrs. Buzzwell and Felicity Jones and Henry Brown went in and out of the hotel. Mr. Brown stood on the sidewalk awhile, talking to Officer Feeney. Mrs. Buzzwell went up and down the street talking to people she met, and even though Bernie couldn't hear a word she said, he knew she was telling them about the latest body at the Bessledorf.

Once the police inspector came back to the hotel and asked to talk to Bernie himself. He wanted to know how Bernie had found the body that morning there on the bed. Bernie told him all he could, except for the part about sticking Hildegarde's hatpin in the corpse's big toe. He did not especially want to hear that on the evening news. Things were bad enough.

Around six o'clock, Bernie finally gave up his post at the second floor window and went down to the lobby. The Magruders were busily preparing for the evening's entertainment in the hotel dining room, and Bernie was proud of his father.

The Magruders were no quitters. They could have, knowing they were sacked, just packed up and left Mr. Fairchild in the lurch. They could have canceled the Cat's Pajamas and left a dining room full of disappointed customers.

"No," said Mr. Magruder, "we gave our word, and we shall keep it. We may be out on the sidewalk come Sunday, or we may be in Ohio; but tonight, the show will go on."

When the news came on, everyone gathered around the television set in the lobby. Mrs. Verona put aside the apple tarts she'd been making and wiped her hands on her apron. Hopkins, the round-faced waiter, stopped nibbling the chocolate off the French coffee cake. Wilbur Wilkins, the handyman, stuck his hammer in his side pocket and stood in front of the television with Henry Brown and all the regulars.

"Good evening," said the announcer. "A third mysterious body turned up today at the ill-fated Bessledorf Hotel in downtown Middleburg, and this time the body did not get away. Called to the hotel by the manager, who found a corpse in an otherwise unoccupied room, the police discovered that the body in residence was that of a missing corpse from the Bessledorf Funeral Parlor next door. The man was returned safely to the mortuary in time for his own funeral, but the fate of the Bessledorf Hotel is in question. Asked about the missing bodies, only one of which had been found, the hotel manager, Theodore Magruder, had no comment, but the police are continuing the investigation."

Mr. Fairchild, who had watched the newscast from the back of the lobby, tapped his cane impatiently on the floor and strode back out into the night.

20

Hopkins

The Cat's Pajamas arrived in pajamas. Theodore Magruder was shocked.

"Joseph, what are you thinking of?" he asked.

"What does it matter?" Joseph said to his father. "We're sacked anyway. If they're going to laugh at us, we'll give them something to laugh about."

They *did* look ridiculous, Bernie decided. The saxophone player had on green-striped pajamas with brown buttons down the front. The trumpeter had on a pair of red polka dots, the drummer wore shorties, his bony knees sticking out the bottoms, and Joseph wore a pair of gray flannels with a "trapdoor" in back. When they gathered in the coatroom before the performance, Mr. Fairchild, who had been standing near the door of the dining room, had to sit down on the first available chair.

It had been an uneventful evening up until now. Bernie took a sandwich to Georgene in the lobby and another to Weasel, who was still sitting on the wall in the alley. The boys discovered that by standing on their skateboards under Henry Brown's window, they could just see over the sill. There wasn't much to see, however. Henry Brown sat reading a newspaper. Every so often he checked his watch, then read some more, then checked his watch again.

"Nothing's happening here," Bernie said at last when it was almost time for the Cat's Pajamas to play. "Why don't you and Georgene come in the dining room for the performance? We might need you more in there."

So Georgene and Weasel took seats near the back.

As had happened the previous weekend, the

dining room was packed and a line formed again in the lobby. Lester, disappointed that he had missed out on all the excitement the week before, put Mixed Blessing in the cellar with the cats but refused to stay with them himself. Every now and then a mournful howl would sweep the lobby.

Salt Water, left as usual as watchbird, greeted ladies with his "Shake a leg," and said, "Hello, Jack," to all the men. People stopped to talk to him, and he strutted cockily back and forth on this perch.

The Bessledorf was obviously *the* place to go on a weekend now, even if nobody stayed in the rooms but the regulars. Bernie heard guests talking about it as they sat down at the tables, or joking about it as they entered the lobby.

"Well, Howard, think you'll be the next to disappear?" one would say to another.

And the other man would laugh and answer, "If I leave the table and don't come back, better go looking for me."

Sometimes, as Bernie passed between tables,

helping out, someone would tap his arm and offer him a dollar to show them the room where the corpse had been found—a fiver if he'd show them all three. Bernie always refused. He wasn't about to make a profit off the Bessledorf's misfortune. But later he discovered Lester leading a tour through the third-floor hallway with a lighted candle and sent him to the basement until the band was ready to perform.

It was time at last. Mr. Fairchild sat expectantly at a table in the center of the room, pleased at the large crowd. Bernie went behind the curtain and dimmed the house lights, turned on the spotlight, and then Delores stepped up on stage.

"Ladies and gentlemen," she said, and this time her voice seemed to choke up a little because she knew it might be the last time she announced the evening's entertainment. "The Bessledorf Hotel is pleased to announce this week's guest attraction, the Cat's Pajamas, a delightful Dixieland combo. Let's welcome them up onstage—the Cat's Pajamas!"

People turned as they heard footsteps coming through the doorway, and when they saw Joseph and his three friends, all dressed up in pajamas, they burst into delighted laughter.

Joseph stood at the microphone and explained how he and his friends were students at the veterinary college and how this was the first time they had performed in public but that there had to be a first time for everything. The people laughed again.

The four young men sat down in the folding chairs on stage. The drummer tapped his foot, nodded his head, and with a "One, and a two, and a three . . ." the music began.

Maybe it was the friendly mood of the crowd, Bernie thought, but the Cat's Pajamas had certainly improved. Once in a while the saxophone player blew a wrong note, and when he did, the drummer made a face. This made the audience laugh again, and the more they laughed, the better the musicians seemed to play. By the time the first number was over, feet were tapping all over the dining room, heads were nodding, hands were clapping, and Mr. Fairchild was smiling broadly.

If only all the bodies hadn't happened, Bernie was thinking. If only the Magruders could start again. He was happier in Middleburg than he had ever been anywhere else. This was the first place he had ever felt at home, and he wanted to stay. If he could just find out why bodies kept disappearing, and have the answer before Sunday. . . .

It was in the middle of the second number that Bernie noticed Hopkins, the round-faced waiter, slip quietly out of the kitchen with a covered tray in his hands, the kind of tray that went to someone who ordered room service. Bernie frowned to himself. Who would be asking for room service now? He peeped out at the audience. Mr. Lamkin was there; Mrs. Buzzwell was there; Felicity Jones was sitting at table by the stage, dreamily watching the saxophone player.

Bernie scanned the audience again. Henry Brown was missing. He had not come to the evening's performance and had evidently ordered dinner in his room.

The music went on. Bernie turned the spotlight from red to blue and back to red again. He was just about to turn up the house lights at the end of the second number when suddenly Hopkins came rushing back through the lobby and burst through the door of the dining room, his face as white as a boiled egg.

"I didn't do it!" he gasped.

Everyone turned.

"I didn't do it! I didn't kill him!" Hopkins went on. "He's dead—the man in 114. Dead as a mackerel!"

And with that, Hopkins fell forward in a faint across Mr. Fairchild's table.

21

Beer and Sweatshirts

Everyone seemed to rise from their seats at once.

"A body! Another body at the Bessledorf!"

Mr. Fairchild lifted the limp Hopkins from off the apple tarts and propped him in a chair, then dashed down the hall toward room 114, followed by Mr. Magruder.

But Bernie knew what he should do. Jumping off the side of the stage, he pushed his way through the tables and over to where Georgene and Weasel were standing.

"The window!" he whispered, and they dashed through the lobby and out the front door. Mrs. Magruder had gone immediately to the phone on the front desk and already Bernie could here the whine of a police siren coming down Main Street.

"You go that way, I'll head him off at this end," Bernie yelled. Georgene and Weasel ran one way around the hotel toward the alley while Bernie ran the other.

As he reached the alley, Bernie heard the hum of a skateboard. He stepped back just in time, for Weasel's skateboard went rolling past him as though an unseen phantom were riding it.

Turning the corner, Bernie saw a man running toward him and, without stopping to think twice, he made a flying tackle for the man's legs.

Whomp! Down they went, the man on top of Bernie, and it felt as though a bag of cement had landed on his back. For a moment Bernie could not breathe, the breath knocked out of his lungs. The man was getting up, swearing, but Bernie could not seem to move. He felt paralyzed. Then, *whomp!* The man fell on top of Bernie again, and then something landed on top of the man. Bernie knew without looking that it was Weasel.

Then there was Georgene's voice yelling, "I've got him! I've got him by the hair!" But her voice ended in a shriek.

At that moment the beam of a police spotlight shone from one end of the alley as a cruiser came roaring up and squealed to a stop.

"Freeze!" yelled Officer Feeney, as the man rolled off Bernie.

Slowly Bernie sat up. A huge crowd had gathered behind the hotel, and Mr. and Mrs. Magruder were running down the alley toward him.

Bernie turned around. Two skateboards were lying upside down there in the alley. A man was sitting on the concrete, a policeman standing on either side of him, but it was no one Bernie knew. He had dark hair and a plain face, but there, dangling from one ear, were the remains of a fake blond beard, and lying on the ground beside him was the black eye patch. Bernie looked at Georgene. She was holding a blond wig in her hands.

Henry Brown!

Just as Mr. and Mrs. Magruder reached Bernie,

Officer Feeney shone a flashlight on the man's face.

"Jackson Prather!" gasped Bernie's parents together.

Bernie stumbled to his feet. He did not know whether to kick the man in the shins or run over and grab hold of his mother. When he looked at his mother, however, she did not look as though she were about to run off with anyone, for she held tightly onto her husband's arm.

"Do you know this man, lady?" asked one of the officers.

"Yes," said Mrs. Magruder softly. "I did once—long ago."

"You son-of-a-gun," said Father to Jackson Prather.

"Now what's all this about?" asked Feeney, as the four members of the Cat's Pajamas made their way through the crowd. "The funny farm, that's what I've got on my beat."

But Jackson Prather was glaring at Bernie's father.

"If it wasn't for those blasted skateboards outside

my window, Magruder, I would have had your job and your wife as well."

"What?" gasped Father.

Jackson Prather got to his feet, wiping the knees of his trousers and the seat of his pants. "You've been bad luck to me all my life, Theodore, and I was about to get even. First you took my girl, then you took my job . . ."

"Jackson Prather?" said Mr. Fairchild, pushing his way past Bernie and facing Mrs. Magruder's old boyfriend. "Officer, this is the man I was about to hire as new manager of my hotel. I almost hired him a year ago but decided on Magruder instead. Then, when all those bodies started to disappear, I thought I'd made a mistake. Now I'm not so sure."

"I lost out to you twenty-three years ago with Alma," said Jackson Prather, still glaring at Mr. Magruder, "and I lost out a year ago when I applied for manager of this hotel. I wasn't about to lose out to you again." He turned to Mother. "Alma, you *would* have gone off with me, wouldn't you?"

"Wrong," said Mother. "You may have let me sit on your jacket once in a canoe, and you may have brought me chocolates in a gold-and-silver box, and you may have whispered in my ear on the porch swing, but I'd never leave my Theodore, not even if we went to the poorhouse."

"My dear, do you mean it?" asked Theodore.

"Of course," said Mother. "I might not have gone to Ohio with you, but then, I wouldn't have let you go there either. We'll go to the poorhouse, Theodore, before we live with your bubblehead of a sister."

Officer Feeney turned to Jackson Prather. "I'm going to take you in for questioning," he said. "It is my duty to inform you that any statements you make may be held against you, and it is your right to have a lawyer present."

"Lawyer, schmawyer," said Jackson Prather as the police handcuffed him. "I want to make a statement anyway. You are looking at Phillip A. Gusset, alias Ethel King, alias Henry Brown, and I do make a good actor if I say so myself. Only problem I had was getting that body out of the funeral parlor and in through a hotel window, but it being all stiff, you know, I just pushed him through feet first."

"Phillip A. Gusset? Ethel King?" said Mr. Magruder, puzzled.

Then Mrs. Magruder gasped and said, "Heliotrope! It must have been his aftershave, Theodore. I *knew* that smell was familiar. I remember it after all these years."

"It may have been heliotrope to you, my dear," said her husband, "but it reminded me of beer and old sweatshirts. I used to play on the same soccer team as Jackson and remember him from the locker room. Never *did* like the man, especially the way he was always sweet-talking you."

"You know," said Mother. "I think you're right. I think maybe it *does* remind me of old sweatshirts after all."

A photographer ran up at that moment and was about to take a picture of Officer Feeney leading Jackson Prather away, but Mr. Magruder stopped him.

"It wasn't Feeney who caught the body snatcher. It was my Bernie." He said. "You want to take a picture, you've got to have him in it."

"Georgene and Weasel helped, too," said Bernie, so all three of them lined up in front of Jackson Prather, who was scowling rather fiercely, while flashbulbs popped and people cheered.

"And write that we caught him with skate-boards," Bernie told one of the reporters. If he couldn't make *The Guinness Book of World Records* for traveling the farthest on a skateboard, maybe he could get in some other way.

Mr. Fairchild walked up to Father and shook his hand. "Magruder," he said, "I want you to go on being manager of my hotel. I've been watching you, and I know that nobody else would have stayed around to keep things going after he'd been sacked. You're all right. What's more, I'm going to hire a professional combo to play in my dining room on Friday and Saturday nights, so you folks don't have to worry about entertainment. And may I take this opportunity to say that you and your family have performed above and beyond the call of duty."

There was more cheering from the people who were watching, the regulars loudest of all.

At that moment the members of the Cat's Pajamas started a tune, and as Feeney stared in disbelief, the musicians in their strange pajamas led a parade up the alley to the tune of "When the Saints Go Marching In." Up the alley, around the corner, past the bus depot, and back into the front entrance of the Bessledorf Hotel, where Mrs. Verona served apple tarts to everyone, and Mr. Fairchild said it was on the house.

And it *was* a house now, Bernie thought happily, as he settled down between his parents for a second helping. It was not only a hotel and a house, it was home.